Adventure Hou
Presents

SPICY ADVENTURE STORIES

November 1939

This reprint edition is a facsmile edition. Variations in print and quality are mostly attributable to the rough woodpulp original this reprint edition is based on.

ISBN: 1-59798-025-0

Published by Adventure House
914 Laredo Road
Silver Spring, Md 20901
www.adventurehouse.com
sales@adventurehouse.com

SPICY-ADVENTURE STORIES

NOVEMBER, 1939 Vol. 11, No. 1

CONTENTS

SPICY-ADVENTURE STORIES is published monthly by the CULTURE PUBLICATIONS, Inc. Editorial offices, 900 Market St., Wilmington, Del. The publisher assumes no responsibility for the return of unsolicited manuscripts.

Never-Never

The boomerang crushed the skull of one of the girl's kidnapers.

THE trail, imperceptible to a white man's eyes even in the daytime let alone this late at night, ended abruptly in a plain of saltbush and whispering grass. Under the cold and distant stars that winked like flung diamonds against the bluish purple of the sky, Corporal Ted Walton, late of Texas and now a member of the South Australian Mounted Police, dismounted from his sorrel gelding and cast a penetrating glance at his black tracker, Bill-Big-Ears. "You savvy him fella Constable Perry stop longa here?"

"Stop longa here, yes. Him fella die longa here, too," Bill-Big-Ears answered out of the velvet darkness as he squatted on his lean bare haunches like a hunkering and frizzy-haired ebony statue.

Walton's mount whickered loudly, then sneezed. A bush rat scurried through the parched undergrowth, making eery rustling noises. In the distance a lone dingo, crippled perhaps, complainingly howled after its pack. Sheep-smell was on the stirring breeze, and nearby a restless bellwether raised its plaintive baa-aa-a at the scent of strange humans.

Corporal Walton shivered and experienced a premonitory sense

Corpses

By ROBERT L. BELLEM

There was plenty of reason for Lisbeth and her father to hate policemen, yet Corporal Walton of the Australian bush patrol wanted to be their friend. But it had passed that point where sheep-stealing was the only trouble. Constable Perry had been bushwhacked and the abbos had tasted kidney fat!

of lurking danger. "You say him police fella Perry die longa here?" he growled sharply. "How you savvy? You talka police fella killed by black boys, eatum kidney fat?"

A week before, Constable Joe Perry had set forth from Walton's lonely outpost station in the Never-Never, on regular bush patrol. Two frigid evenings later his horse had returned, riderless, with blood on the reins. With Bill-Big-Ears, Ted Walton had set out to find him—or to see what had become of him. Now he was finding out, and what he was learning filled him with dark gusts of anger.

"Bush fella no killum, no eatum kidney fat," Bill-Big-Ears said flatly. "Track showum no black boy, no lubra. Just police fella Perry longa 'nother white fella. Other white fella sneak up, shoot-um police fella, me tellum true. Perry, hide um grave under salt-bush. You look." He pointed to a disturbed sector of earth that had recently been a low mound.

It was amazing the way the *abbo* tracker could read the dim trail signs and from them reconstruct the thing that had happened. Walton moved grimly forward, drew out his flashlight and flared it. What he saw sent nausea churning into his belly—and he was a strong man, accustomed to violence.

All that was left of Constable Joe Perry lay hideously in a depression scooped out of the brick-hard ground. The raw and scalpless skull was shattered, front and back, by the vicious passage of a rifle bullet.

"Bushwhacked!" Walton muttered through clenched teeth. "The killer didn't even have kindness enough to do a decent job of burial. Stuck him in a shallow hole so the dingoes could get at him, by God!"

It was true enough. Wild dogs had scratched and clawed at the makeshift grave, uncovered the slain man's corpse and feasted horribly on it. Tonight, had not Walton come, they would certainly have returned to finish their meal . . .

Walton set his flashlight on a boulder. "You fella dig deeper hole, cover police fella Perry with stones. I'm going nosing around a bit." He strode into the darkness, scowling, swearing in his tight throat.

Up the dry wash, disturbed sheep milled nervously to the tinkle of a lead-ram's bell. Walton saw the woollen sea of movement before him—but he didn't notice the flittering shadow behind him. Not until a feminine voice said: "I've got you covered, lamb-killer. Turn around, slowly." A flash-ray speared the blackness as Walton pivoted. The light bathed him. And the feminine voice gasped: "Ted—*you!*"

"Lisbeth," he said. "Lisbeth McBaine."

IN THE flashlight's reflected glow she was like a lithe young goddess clad in walking-boots, short whipcord skirt and caressing silken blouse that limned the nubile contours of her swelling breasts. Like spun mahogany was the wavy heaviness of her hair, and her lips seemed to brim with crimson kisses. But her eyes were hard with a counterfeit hardness.

"We don't want policemen on our land," she said tonelessly.

"That doesn't apply to me, surely?"

"You're a policeman." Bitterness stole into her voice, and her ripe lips curled with contempt.

He knew how she felt toward the law. He didn't blame her, much. Her father had served three years in Melbourne prison for a shooting scrape—a scrape he could scarcely have avoided, since it was forced on him by a drunk. But Dominion law was stern, and old Dan McBaine had done his time, and during his absence his daughter had been forced to make shift as best she could with the sheep. It had been all the harder for her because there'd been a drought year that wiped out half her flocks, and she hadn't been able to hire help.

Loving her, hoping one day to marry her, Ted Walton had wanted to throw his lot with hers. He'd even offered to resign his post, work for her as overseer. But she'd have none of it. Her father's imprisonment had done something to her; had changed and embittered her against the law and its uniformed servants. She seemed to feel that the old man's sentence had been unjust; that the arresting officer could as easily have turned him loose, knowing that the gunfight was not of Dan's picking. And old Dan himself, now that he was back from jail, was of a simillar mind. "Stay off our place," he had warned Walton. "You and your men stay clear. Understand?"

But it was different now. Ted Walton had a duty to perform—a duty he didn't like. Yet it faced him, for all his inner unwillingness. He was remembering that the murdered Constable Perry had been the officer who'd arrested old Dan McBaine in Melbourne, a little over three years ago. . . .

"Listen, Lisbeth," he said, stepping toward her. "Put away your gun. And tell me why you pulled it on me."

"We've been losing sheep lately. I heard them bawling, and I thought you—"

He shook his head. "I'm no lamb-killer. I'm here for a different reason. There's been a murder. One of my constables. On your land."

"A p-policeman . . . killed?" She seemed to wilt, to grow suddenly fearful. Then she squared her shoulders. "We don't know anything about it. The man had no business inside our boundaries anyhow."

Walton said: "I wouldn't try that attitude if I were you, Lisbeth. It was Constable Perry."

"J-Joe Perry—? Oh, my God!" The last of her reserve broke. She crumpled against Walton's muscular form and shuddered in his encircling arms. He could feel the flattened pressure of her breasts on his drill shirt, the trembling of her young body. A tingling thrill coursed into him; it had been many a weary day since she'd been this close to him, and his veins thrummed with longing. Her lips fluttering to his cheek, she whispered: "You d-don't think my father . . . did it? You *can't* think that! I won't let you! He's innocent!"

"Perry took your dad to jail. Some men are vengeful."

"Not my father! You know him better than that. Oh-h-h, Ted . . .!" She melted against him miserably; and her upturned, tremulous lips were a sweet temptation in the starlight. He lowered his mouth toward them, because he couldn't help himself.

HARD fingers sank into his shoulders, unexpectedly, just as he was bending the girl far backward in his embrace. He was spun around, off-balance. Lisbeth, released, fell sprawling in the dry grass, her abbreviated whipcord skirt's hem fluttering upward to disclose an enticing hint of bare white skin below glove-silk panties. Even as she cried out, a bashing fist took Ted Walton on the chin. He sagged; was struck again, solidly. He pitched forward on his face, stunned, with the taste of his own blood salty in his mouth.

His reflexes made him squirm aside to miss the lashing impact of a heavy boot in his ribs. The kick grazed him. Then Lisbeth wailed: "No, Stephen! No! *Please!*"

Walton scrambled groggily to his feet. He saw facing him a huge, towering man in corduroys; a man who outweighed him a good thirty pounds, whose fists were like footballs, whose features were venomously contorted by fury. Instinctively, Walton's hand dropped to his holstered gun.

Then he grinned redly. He didn't need bullets to teach this big hulk a lesson. "Hit me when I'm unprepared, will you?" he said softly. "Okay, laddybuck. Try it again—if you dare." He crouched; moved forward.

The bigger man snarled: "I saw you trying to make love to Lisbeth—forcing yourself on her. I'll kill you." He swung.

Walton rode with the punch; started to counter. But Lisbeth sailed through the darkness to interpose herself. "Stop it! Stop it, both of you! I won't let you fight!"

"Afraid I might hurt him?" Walton asked quietly.

"Never mind my reasons. You shan't fight."

"And just who is this chap you're so interested in protecting?"

The big man answered for himself, hotly. "None of your sarcasm, you blinking tin soldier. I don't need Lisbeth to protect me. I can take care of myself—and her too. Since you wanted to know, I'll tell you who I am. I'm Steve Trenlawn, and I'm overseer of this layout for Lisbeth's father—

"And Steve and I are going to be married soon," Lisbeth interrupted.

It was like a knife twisting in Walton's heart. He could understand, now, why Trenlawn had attacked him. "Sorry," he said shortly to the bigger man. He offered his hand. "No hard feelings. And . . . felicitations to you both."

Trenlawn ignored the proffered handshake. "Stow it," he snarled. "And take yourself off this land."

"Afraid I can't do that until I've questioned McBaine," Walton said. He looked at the girl. "Will you lead the way to the house?"

Trenlawn was truculent. "What the devil do you want to question him about? What's up?"

"Murder," Walton snapped. "Let's go."

THE HOUSE was a half-mile up the wash, resting upon a rolling knoll in a blue-gum thicket. Single file they traversed the distance, with Lisbeth leading; and Walton felt a gnawing emptiness in him when he watched the erect lilt of her shoulders, the feminine sway of her supple hips. Once she'd belonged to him, he'd thought. Now he had lost her. She was going to marry Trenlawn. It would be Trenlawn, and not Ted Walton, who would harvest kisses from her moist lips and know the intimate glories of her body. . . .

Off beyond the blue-gum a *buk-buk* owl screamed as it made a

"Please don't put my father under arrest!" she pleaded.

bush-rat kill. To the right of the rambling sod-and-thatch ranch house, campfires burned against the darkness where a cluster of semi-wild abbos and their lubras nested for the night, their womeras and boomerangs and spears near at hand. Hired for the seasonal sheep-shearing, Walton thought; although it was strange that old Dan McBaine would employ bushmen so obviously close to aboriginal savagery when mission-schooled blacks could be had for the asking. But maybe these natives could be engaged more cheaply, since McBaine was short on funds; with which thought, the corporal dismissed the matter from his mind. He had other and more important matters to consider.

McBaine himself was waiting in the barely-furnished front room of the house. He glared rheumily as Walton entered. "You!" he snorted. "So you decided to take a hand in the matter yourself, did you? It's blasted near time."

"What matter?" Walton raised his brows.

"The sheep-stealing and lamb-killing, of course! Don't tell me that Perry blighter didn't report it to you? I met him four or five days ago; gave him the whole story. Wild abbos have been butchering my stock, running it off . . . What's wrong with your face? And why stare at me that way?"

Walton gingerly touched his fist-bruised lips and cast a warning shake of the head at Steve Trenlawn. "Never mind my face, sir. You say you reported your trouble to Constable Perry four days ago?"

"Four or five. What does it matter? I told him everything—including the disappearance of Mo-bo, my 'breed herder."

"Perry never had the chance to report to me," Walton said. "He was bushwhacked. I just discovered his body—on your land."

The old man paled. "Murdered? Good God . . ." Suddenly the full force of the disclosure seemed to dawn on him. "You don't suspect *me* of—?"

"It's not my business to accuse, sir. That's up to the authorities. My job is to take you in for questioning. I'm sorry. But you see how it is. The circumstances . . ."

"Damn the circumstances! I won't go with you! I'll see you in hell first!"

"Daddy!" Lisbeth cried softly. "It won't be for long. You can clear yourself easily. Steve and I can . . . run things while you're gone. And if . . . if anything goes wrong, we can take the wool money to hire a barrister . . ." She seemed to be imploringly signaling her father; Walton didn't miss the hidden undercurrent of her glance.

Trenlawn took it up. "She's right, Dan. Best go quietly with our tin-soldier friend. Things will work out."

The old man's shoulders sagged. "Very well. Are we starting now?"

OUT in the bush, a scared wallaby raced through the night with a series of diminishing thump-sounds. From the abbo camp drifted the smell of seared kangaroo-meat held over live coals. Walton shook his head. "We'll trek at sun-up if it's all the same to you. Mind putting me up for the night?"

"You can blanket down here in the living room if you've a mind to," McBaine growled ungraciously. "Come on, Lisbeth. And you, Steve. Let's go to bed."

They left Walton alone in the room, his only light a dull glow from the fireplace. He unrolled his blanket, spread it and settled himself on the hard floor. After a while, he dozed.

It was dark when he felt the touch of a hand on his face. He tensed; reached for his holstered gun. Then he relaxed as he heard Lisbeth's soft whisper: "Ted . . . darling . . ."

The hearth-coals had died to ash. He sensed, rather than saw, that Lisbeth was clad only in nightgown and filmy negligee. The fragrance of her hair drifted to his nostrils like tantalizing wine; her unexpected nearness sent ripples of yearning through him. "What's wrong?" he answered, sitting up and seizing her hand.

"N-nothing . . . except that I couldn't sleep. Oh, Ted . . . please don't put my f-father under arrest! He didn't k-kill Joe Perry; he w-wouldn't!"

"If he's innocent, he'll go free. I'm not the judge, Lisbeth. It's my duty to take him in."

"Does a police officer always think only of duty? Never of . . . anything else?"

Her skin was smooth and cool to his touch; in the deep gloom he knew that the swift intake of her breath had enticingly pouted out the twin mounds of her breasts against clinging silk and lace. In his mind's eye he pictured those unseen charms that were so close to him, and a sudden feverish desire laid hold of his soul, blinding him to everything save the possibilities of the moment.

His arm went about her pliant waist and he drew her against his throbbing body, crushing her with an ardent intensity that seemed to kindle and ignite responsive spates of flame in her own heart. She parted her sweetly-surrendered lips for his seeking kiss . . .

"Ted . . .!" she moaned as he caressed her. "It's been so long . . . and so lonely . . . ah, Ted . . .!"

He stormed his mouth at her eyes, her cheeks, the lovely hollow of her flawless throat. "Lisbeth!" he whispered fiercely, "You belong to me—not to that Trenlawn chap! You're mine, understand? *Mine!*" His fingers danced along her arms.

She made no verbal answer; but her warm arms locking about his neck told him all he needed to know. She fused herself to him with pagan fervor; whimpered ecstatically under the thrill of his straying kisses . . .

THEN something happened; something that destroyed the spell. Someone had thrown a handful of pebbles against the window. A sibilant hiss reached Walton's ears.

He froze; frowned. That would be Bill-Big-Ears. The black tracker's hissing signal had come to him many a time in the past—and always it meant danger, the necessity for speedy action. "Damn!" he whispered as he started to get up on his feet.

Lisbeth tried to hold him. "Don't go . . . now. Please . . ."

"I must." He disengaged her arms from around his neck. He went to the open window. "What is it?" he called quietly.

Bill-Big-Ears crouched outside the sill. "White fella old man go longa out of here bimeby just now. Sneak into bush, run fast away."

Walton stiffened. "So that's it!" he rasped as he swung around to face Lisbeth in the darkness. "You were playing a game—keeping me busy while your father pulled an escape. Nice."

She flung herself on him. "Ted . . . Ted . . . I admit that was my plan. But after you k-kissed me, I . . . I forgot such things."

He turned away from her, bitterly. Bill-Big-Ears was talking again. "You come quick. Me fella findum something longa here you wantum see. Findum fella 'breed longa bush, fella dead man, dingoes eatum kidney fat, you come look."

Another dead man! Corporal Ted Walton's fists clenched into steel-hard hammers of wrath. Without a word he leaped out through the open window. "You showum-me—fast!" he whispered.

Bill-Big-Ears scuttled off into the blue-gum thicket, as soundlessly as a black ghost. Walton followed. A mile beyond the knoll, they halted by a saltbush clump. A startled brush-turkey took wing into the night, its pinions drumming weirdly against the stillness. "Look," the tracker pointed. He produced Walton's flashlight and triggered it.

In the round white glare, the corporal saw a disturbed mound similar to the spot where he'd found Constable Perry's mutilated corpse. And now he was gazing at another dead man—a half-breed, from the color of the few shreds of skin still clinging to the fang-peeled bones. Here again the dingoes had feasted revoltingly; and Walton choked back the oath that leaped to his lips.

"This must be that 'breed herder McBaine mentioned as missing—the chap he called Mo-bo. And dead a day or more ahead of Perry, from the looks of him. Shot through the back of the head and left for the dingoes. They've eaten more of him than they did of Perry—which places this murder before the other one."

Bill-Big-Ears nodded wisely. "Him police fella Perry stop longa here, see um fella dead man, go 'way—and gettum fella self bushwhacked down longa dry wash, later. Me fella read signs, tellum true."

Walton stared. "Constable Perry discovered this corpse? And later was ambushed? Good God—then we know why Perry was murdered. It was because he'd seen too much! He might even have guessed the identity of the killer!"

A lot of that was over Bill-Big-Ears' frizzy head, but he seemed to catch its general import. He nodded rapidly. "Me first class fella tracker. Me readum signs. Savvy plenty longa this place. Savvy fella old man, white missy's father, savvy him no killum herder, no killum fella Perry."

"Say that again—slowly!" Walton barked. "You mean Old Dan McBaine isn't the murderer?"

Bill-Big-Ears grinned, his white teeth showing against the solid black of his features. "Savvy fella white man stealum sheep, drive um away, killum lambs. Fella 'breed herder see um, make talka-talk. Fella white man killum 'breed herder, you bet my life."

IT WAS clearing up now. A white sheep-stealer, and not wild bush abbos, had been plunder-

With that blow Ted knew he had broken his hand.

ing the McBaine flocks. And Mo-bo the half-caste herder, had caught the man red-handed.

Then the murderer had buried his victim shallowly, for the prowling dingoes. And along had come Constable Joe Perry, who must have smelled out the truth.

Obviously, then, Dan McBaine wasn't guilty. He wouldn't have been rustling his own sheep. Nor would Lisbeth. And there were no other whites in this sector of the Never-Never—unless it be a stray outlaw marauder from the bush over Stuart Range way. That was possible, but—

"You fella Bill!" Walton snapped grimly. "You top fella tracker. You tellum me 'bout trail-signs, footprints. You tellum fella me, name fella bushwhacker —quick. You savvy?"

Bill-Big-Ears nodded and grinned. "Me savvy. Him fella big white overseer, him wear fella boots, make mark like so." He drew a crescent on the disturbed earth, using the point of a gum-wood splinter. "You catchum."

"Damned right I'll catchum. Come on, Bill. We're going to put the neck-irons on Steve Trenlawn!"

Out of the darkness came words. "Not by half, tin soldier. Dead men don't put neck-irons on any-body—and you're a dead man." A gun blasted the night, its muzzle-flame spitting at the velvet darkness.

But Ted Walton had already flung himself sidewise. Now he rolled frantically, Trenlawn's whistling slug slamming past him in a clean miss. Bill-Big-Ears yelped and crab-scuttled to the protection of the surrounding bush as Trenlawn fired again.

Walton jerked at his holstered gun. The flap was buttoned, and it stuck. He cursed as his fingers fought the recalcitrant leather.

It was his curses that enabled Trenlawn to spot him. The big man spanked another slug at him. Walton rolled again, his eyes smarting from bullet-thrown sand. And Trenlawn was shouting: "Sure I rustled the sheep—for a good reason. You'll damned soon find it out, too. I intended to break McBaine—take his ranch away from him, and his girl as well. Too bad my plans went astray—but I was hoping maybe you'd nab the old man for those killings. That would have done just as well. Once I was left alone with her—" He fired a third time.

He missed.

WALTON had his own gun out now. He aimed and squeezed lead at the flame-stab before him. Trenlawn yelped like a maniac; dropped his automatic. The corporal's slug had clipped the weapon square, dashed it from his grasp. Now, his hand paralyzed by the shock of that nerve-shattering concussion, the bigger man danced around in roaring pain.

Walton moved forward cautiously, straining his eyes. "Stand still or I'll let you have it instead of going to the trouble of dragging you into post in chains!" he growled.

Then he froze stock-still. From somewhere nearby there came a wailing scream. Lisbeth McBain's shrill cry, burdened with terror! "Ted! Oh, God — Ted — *help me*—!"

Out of the gloom came Trenlawn's sinister laugh. "I'm still holding trumps, tin soldier. That's my blacks—the abbos you saw camped near the house. *My* abbos, tin soldier. The ones I gave fresh meat to. The ones I'm using to win my game for me. Get that? I told 'em to grab Lisbeth. Well, they've got her. If you kill me, you know damned well what they'll do to her—and you won't be able to stop 'em. They'll be gone in the bush before you can get on their trail. A white lubra will be a new kind of playtoy to 'em . . ."

"You filthy, stinking swine!"

Walton whispered hoarsely. "They wouldn't dare! You wouldn't let them—"

"They're obeying my orders, tin soldier."

"Then call to them, damn you! Tell them to drop her! Tell them before I blow your dirty guts through your spine!"

Again the bigger man chortled. "I'll tell them when you hand over your gun. Not before. Step alive —if you want to save Lisbeth."

Walton hesitated. Cold sweat formed in his armpits. Trenlawn spoke truth: he held trump cards. To shoot him down in cold blood wouldn't help Lisbeth. Those semi-savage abbos would whisk her into the bush as quick as a wink—unless they were stopped by Trenlawn's command. And a dead Trenlawn would issue no such order. Neither would a live Trenlawn—unless Walton surrendered his gun.

The man was a bestial monster. He didn't care a fig what happened to Lisbeth—as long as he could save his own scummy neck. "Do I get your gun, tin soldier?" he sneered.

Walton cursed Bill-Big-Ears for deserting him, But that was the way with blacks; the mission-schooled ones, anyhow. They didn't like to mix into white men's fights. As trackers they had no equal. But as fighters against members of the dominant race—no. Pit them against their own kind and it was a different story. If only Bill-Big-Ears had sense enough to—

(Continued on page 101)

A pounding at the door! Emy tried to get loose. "Leave me here. Save yourself!"

GLORY'S EPITAPH

By JEROME SEVERS PERRY

In Nazi Czechoslovakia, Jett Kenthorne finds danger and espionage, a mysterious knife, and a girl to whom some things mean more than life itself . . .

THE FERRET-faced runt was an excellent actor. He pulled an ugly looking pocket knife out of his pants, opened up the biggest blade, and came winging across the *bierstube* at me. His beady eyes glittered and his lips were peeled back from protruding front teeth in a snarl. *"Schweinkopf!"* he yelled. "I'll slice your Yankee gullet to mincemeat!"

I kicked a chair aside to give me room for action, and I balled my fists. Three bulky Prussians at an adjoining table put down their steins and stopped talking among themselves. In fact, everybody in the *bierstube* fell silent except for the cute little blue-eyed blonde girl who had been warbling at the tin-pan piano. She screamed faintly and pressed her hand against a pouting mound of her snowy breast—a mound that swelled gorgeously from the squarecut lowness of her decolletage. "No! Please, no! Not on account of me!" she wailed.

She tried to block Ferret-Face as he charged. He shoved her away, roughly. That was what had started it in the first place. He had insisted upon heckling her as she sang her *lieder;* and when that had failed to disturb her, he had gone further. He had put his hands on her, pawed her.

That was when I'd collared him and tossed him bodily against the wall. Now he was scrambling back at me with this big knife in his fist.

HE WAS a Bohemian, but he was cursing me in fluent German as he leaped. There was nothing particularly unusual in that. Prague is a polyglot city anyhow, and since the fall of Czechoslovakia to the Nazis a lot of people had switched over to the tongue of the conquerors merely to show their allegiance to the swastika. And an oath is an oath no matter how you spit it out.

For that matter, a knife is a knife the world over, too. This one looked plenty deadly. The blade was sharp and stainless, the handle wrought of polished brown bone. I ducked the frenzied thrust and made a grab for the runt's thin wrist. I twisted.

He slobbered out an agonized moan and dropped the weapon. I scooped it up, closed it and thrust it into my coat pocket. Then I said in English: "Nobody pulls a shiv on me and gets away with it, buddy. Here's something to remember me by." And I boffed him on the dimple. Not hard, but it looked good to the bystanders.

He went down like a wet rag. I gathered him out of the sawdust, carried him to the front door, and tossed him casually into the darkness of the cobblestoned street. As I did it, I whispered: "Nice work, guy." It was late at night, and no traffic moved in that section of the city, down near the Vltava waterfront. The runt smiled at me as he landed on the sidewalk. Then he scurried toward an adjacent alley.

I was dusting my hands when I turned around and re-entered the *bierstube*. I walked smack-dab into the muzzle of a Mauser automatic.

The man who jammed the Mauser into my midriff was one of the three who had been sitting at the table next to mine. He was a tall, heavyset lug with a military manner, a close-cropped haircut, and a saber scar across his left cheek from eye to chin. He had Prussian scrawled all over him. His two companions backed up his play. They looked Prussian, too. They were army officers in spite of their civilian clothes. I could see that.

The one with the Mauser said: "Consider yourself under arrest, *herr* spy."

I felt a cold tingle racing through my marrow. I didn't like the tone of his voice, and his words sounded damned ominous, considering my real reason for being in Prague. I shook my head and pretended not to understand, although I savvy German as well as the next kraut-eater. "What the hell is the matter with you?" I fired back at him in good old United States lingo. "Put that hog-leg away before it goes off and hurts somebody."

"I am *Oberlieutnant* Von Kragg of the *Gestapo*—the secret police," he growled gutturally. "These are my men. I would advise you not to resist, my American friend."

With that, the cute little blonde songstress darted up to me. Her trim ankles twinkled as she ran, and from the way her lush bosom swayed I could guess she wasn't wearing much under her lowcut evening gown. She jammed herself close to me, so that I could feel the yielding warmth of her bosom against my arm. Her beauty was pulse-stirring, breath-taking; and her nearness sent a thrill into me. She started jabbering in German: "You cannot arrest this American! He did not do anything wrong! He merely interfered when that horrid little man annoyed me, and—"

"Shut your mouth, *fraulein,* before I close it for you with this!" The Prussian held up the flat of his free left hand and made a move to sting it across her face.

She cringed.

I WHAPPED him, Mauser or no Mauser. I put heft behind my knuckles. They connected, and he sat down on the floor in one damned large hurry. Then his two buddies closed in on me like a pair of furies.

They gave me a proper working over before they succeeded in pinioning me. By the same token, I dished out a few black eyes and broken teeth on my own account. And as I fought, I was trying to get hold of that knife in my coat pocket. Not to use it, but to throw it away.

No dice. My two straw-haired assailants backed me into a corner, kicked me in the groin, and finally Von Kragg got up and dusted me off with a beer stein. It was the stein that took the fight out of me. I was barely able to stand on my feet as I panted: "Okay, you lousy sons. But I'm warning you. My name is Jett Kenthorne, I'm an American citizen with my income taxes paid, and I'm going to raise holy hell with my consul about this. Somebody is going to collect a godawful root in the pants for pushing me around this way, mark my words."

Von Kragg's face twisted in an ugly sneer, so that the saber scar writhed like a white tapeworm under his complexion. "Your country will do nothing for you, *Herr* Kenthorne," he said. "We have caught you in an act of deliberate treachery against *Der Fuhrer.*"

"I'm not even acquainted with the guy," I growled.

"Ah. But you *are* acquainted with a certain Gollancz Dresca, a college classmate of yours, years ago, in the United States."

My heart sank. Now I was in for it! I could see trouble coming, hellity-larrup.

Von Kragg said: "Dresca was one of those misguided patriots who attempted to halt the march of empire; who tried to stop us from assuming control of Czechoslovakia. Also, he once saved your life, several years ago."

"So what?" I said.

"In spite of his recent political efforts, we succeeded in effecting *anschluss* with Czechoslovakia; and we placed this Dresca under arrest. You, who happened to be traveling in Europe at the time, heard of his capture and came here to Prague hoping to repay your debt to him; hoping to help him escape the fate which justly awaits him."

"Nuts!" I retorted. It was a weak answer, but the best I could manage under the conditions. Thus far, Von Kragg had been shooting nothing but bull's-eyes, dead center.

HE WENT on: "Last week, just prior to your arrival here, Dresca broke from confinement and got away; has not yet been recaptured. Since then you have been attempting to locate him so that you might spirit him into neutral territory and thus save his life. Do you admit these things?"

"I don't admit anything except that you're a jackass with the plotting instincts of a dime novelist," I said.

He laughed, but it wasn't a pleasant sound to hear. "You hired a number of persons to help you locate Dresca. You arranged that they were to report any findings to you, here in this *bierstube,* by pretending to attack you. You were not aware that one of the men you engaged happens to be a member of the *Gestapo,* and that he has kept me cognizant of your moves."

I felt sick. I hadn't expected that kind of double cross, and I wondered which one of my hastily-assembled outfit had scuttled me.

Von Kragg said: "Tonight, a member of your hirelings came here with important news regarding Dresca's whereabouts. Acting drunk, he insulted a singer—according to your own plan. That gave you a chance to interfere. I was much entertained when you took away his knife after he feigned a desire to cut your throat."

"Feigned, hell!" I lied. "That was the real thing."

The Prussian chuckled. "You cannot fool me, my friend. Unfortunately for him, your pretended attacker is now in the hands of my operatives. They were waiting for him outside when you threw him into the street. And now you, too, are in custody. I will trouble you for that knife, *Herr* Kenthorne."

I was sunk. It was all true. Gollancz Dresca was my best friend, and the ferret-faced runt had been one of my hired hands. If I had unwittingly thrown the runt to the *Gestapo,* his head would roll in the sand as surely as a hangover follows Saturday night. Moreover, if Von Kragg took that knife away from me, I would never know where to locate Dresca. On the contrary, the knife might turn out to be the means whereby Dresca would be captured by his Nazi enemies. Then he, too, would face the headsman's axe—and it would be all my fault.

Yet what could I do? I was held helpless as the Prussians fanned my pockets, dragged out the knife. Von Kragg examined it curiously, wondering where the message might be concealed. "What is the secret?" he demanded. "You had better answer the truth if you know what is good for you."

A wave of mingled relief and dismay shot through me. He didn't have the right knife! This one had a handle of black bone instead of brown, and the blade was blue steel instead of stainless. Somehow a switch had been accomplished. I could think of only one way in which it could possibly have been done. And I knew I had to do some fast moving.

I said: "You're as nutty as a June bug, mister. You won't find any message in that shiv."

He put it on the table, smashed the handle to bits with the bottom of a pewter stein. Then he pulled a magnifying glass from his vest and carefully examined the knife's broken fragments. Naturally, he didn't find anything. And he seemed puzzled.

"Search him thoroughly!" he barked to his two underlings. Which they did—without result.

I said: "Now that you're through, I demand an apology. Or would you sooner have an international incident made of this?"

HE WAS over a barrel. "We are very sorry, *Herr* Kenthorne," he said, clicking his heels together and bowing stiffly from the waist. But his eyes cursed me, told me that I'd be under strict surveillance from then on.

I grinned. Von Kragg and his buddies stalked out. I wandered over to the bar, ordered a fresh mug of Pilsner. To the barkeep I said: "What became of the lady? I'd like to hear some more songs."

"She left. She went home."

I slipped him a gold coin. "What's her address?" And I winked meaningly.

He whispered a street number; added: "You will get nowhere with her. Others have tried it during the week she has worked here. She is not that sort." He leaned toward me. "I can tell you where there are girls just as pretty—" And he named an address.

"No, thanks." I downed my beer; walked out. Sure enough, I saw someone fall into step behind me. But I'm an old hand at shaking shadows. Fifteen minutes later I was in a rooming house on the other side of the river, in Old Town. To the harridan who ran the place I said: "I'm looking for the *fraulein* who sings at the Vltava *Bierstube.*"

"Emy Lohrr? Her room is on the third floor at the head of the stairs." The harridan went back to her burrow. Evidently she didn't care what went on under her roof, as long as the tenants paid their rent.

So the blonde girl's name was Emy Lohrr. It had a nice sound. As I ascended, I kept remembering her blue eyes, her plump curves, her clear voice—and the way she had pressed herself close to me a while ago. That was when she must have picked my pocket, substituted another knife. I didn't understand the play, but she had certainly got me out of a jam. I wanted to thank her—and I wanted that knife.

I knocked on her door. A voice said: "Come in," and I ankled across the threshold to see somebody I wasn't expecting; somebody I didn't know. A brunette girl, tall, willowy, slender and very obviously nervous. She was dressed in a negligee of sheer chiffon that didn't match the room's tawdry shabbiness. Through the chiffon I could see plenty that was interesting. Or rather, they might have interested me if I hadn't been expecting to see someone who owned a plumper collection of charms.

I said: "Excuse me, please. I must have the wrong room. I was looking for Emy Lohrr." And then I noticed something on the bureau. A knife with a brown bone handle and stainless steel blades. A tiny screwdriver lay near it, as if the brunette girl had been on the verge of taking the knife apart.

She smiled. "But this is Emy's room. She—she has gone out."

I reached toward the bureau. "She borrowed this from me. I came to get it back."

"You — you are *Herr* Kenthorne?"

Surprise made me blink. "Yes. How did you know that?"

"I am Gollancz Dresca's sister."

I STIFFENED. It was the first time I'd known he had a sister. I said: "Huh? Then you know all about—?"

"Yes. And Emy took a singing job in that *bierstube* so that she could keep a watch on your progress; help you if necessary. Tonight she helped you very much. Now, *Gott sei dank,* we will find my brother . . ." Tears brimmed in the brunette's eyes. She slid her arms around my neck. "I am so grateful to you for what you have done!" And she kissed me, hard.

I was dumb. I fell for the play. After all, she was a delicious armload, and she was melting against me in a way that got me. I could feel her small, firm bosom burrowing at my shirt-front and her lips parting to the pressure of my mouth. I thought it was her way of displaying gratitude. I soon found out my mistake.

Off to my left, a muffled feminine voice yipped: "Kenthorne—look out!"

I ducked just in time. The blackjack intended for my skull caught me on the shoulder instead. A great big bruiser had sneaked in through the door from the adjoining room, and he was bludgeoning me as if he meant to make jelly of my grey matter. Moreover, the brunette girl was hanging onto me for dear life, impeding my movements and hampering my attempts to defend myself.

Another blow hit me on the arm. I jerked free of the dark-haired girl; gave her a loose-fisted punch that sailed her across the room in a flurry of negligee. She landed on her back with her bare legs kicking. I pivoted; faced the squarehead with the blackjack. He tried to mace me between the eyes. I kicked him, and I didn't care whether my foot landed fair or foul. It landed foul and he folded over, groaning. I straightened him with an uppercut that put him to sleep in a very thorough way.

The brunette scrambled to her feet and came at me. I simply had to tag her, much as I hate to boff a member of the softer gender. Then, when she had gone sprawling across the limp form of the blackjack artist, I made for the next room—where I could hear muffled moans and frantic heel-thumpings.

THe blonde singer from the *bierstube* was tied to a chair. She was all mussed up. Her gown had been torn down the front, revealing plenty of snowy epidermis. There was a bruise on her cheek and a gag in her mouth. She had managed partially to dislodge the gag in order to scream a warning at me.

I untied her, took away the gag. "What the devil is this all about?" I said.

"*I* am Gollancz Dresca's sister," she whimpered. "That other girl lied to you in order to lull your suspicions. I learned that you were going to try to save my brother; I heard about your plans, and I took a job in that *bierstube* so that I could be close to you in case anything happened. Tonight, when the Gestapo arrested you, I managed to sneak that knife from your pocket and replace it with another. Then I came home here to my room. But just as I was about to take the knife apart, that w-woman and her companion j-jumped me . . ."

"So they're secret police!" I muttered. "They've had you under surveillance all the time. Prague must be full of them, by God!"

"Y-yes . . .!"

I said: "Well, we're on top thus far. Maybe we can stay that way. Come on, let's get moving." I grabbed the knife off the bureau, took her hand, and pulled her to the stairs. Nobody blocked us. We gained the street without being seen, as far as I could judge. I made for the ancient, towered stonework of the Charles Bridge.

Emy Lohrr, whose real name I now knew to be Emy Dresca, whispered: "Wh-where are we going?"

"To some hotel where I can read the message in the knife—and then leave you in hiding while I make arrangements to sneak you and your brother out of the country. I don't dare take you to my own hotel. It's undoubtedly being watched by Von Kragg's men."

"*All* hotels are watched by Von Kragg's men. They are infested with spies. The moment we register, we will be betrayed to the *Gestapo!*" she choked.

Then I got a bright idea. I remembered the address which had been mentioned to me by that *bierstube* barkeep when he thought I was looking for an evening's fun. It wasn't very far away, and it might serve my purpose. The proprietors of such places aren't usually any more friendly with the police than they have to be . . .

Five minutes later I knuckled the front door of a ramshackle building, and a purse-bellied Bohemian let us in. He grinned and winked when I told him we wanted temporary accommodations; took my money and led us upstairs to a dingy room. As I closed the door after him, I could hear shrill laughter and tinkling glasses down the hall, and I hated to think of having brought a sweet kid like Emy into that sort of dive. But there was no help for it. And she didn't seem to mind. She realized what we were up against.

I went to work on the knife; took it apart. A tiny spill of tissue paper had been secreted down under the main blade. I unfolded it, held it to the light and read it:

> *"Come to 1567 Josefplatz near the old powder-tower by Celetna ulice promptly at midnight. G. Dresca."*

I recognized the handwriting. It was unquestionably my old friend's; so I knew I wasn't being kidded. But when I looked at my watch I saw that it lacked a good forty minutes of midnight; I had a wait ahead of me.

That wasn't going to be unpleasant. I smiled at Emy. "You don't mind if I stay here instead of roaming the streets and maybe picking up a shadow?"

SHE came close to me, and she didn't seem to realize how much the front of her gown had been torn. "I want you to stay here," she whispered shyly, taking my hand and holding it.

I could look down and glimpse the lovely valley of her swelling bosom; and my heart skipped a couple of beats. I had a sudden insane urge to take her in my arms, squeeze her, kiss her until she panted for breath. There was something about her that stirred me, churned up a lot of emotional seethe within my veins. Maybe some day, when I had pulled her and her brother out of danger. . . .

But not now. It was neither the time nor the place. So I merely pressed her fingers, smiled down into her anxious blue eyes. Then I got busy with sheets and blankets from the bed, twisting them and knotting them together to make an improvised rope. The room's window looked down on an alley behind the house, and that was the way I intended to make my getaway—just in case any of Von Kragg's men happened to be watching the front door.

I DIDN'T quite reckon on his Teutonic thoroughness. When the time came, I blew a kiss at Emy, slid over the windowsill, and lowered myself to the alley. Whereupon I landed in a nest of trouble.

Two burly Prussians dived at me from the darkness. I realized that Emy and I must have been tailed from her rooming house to this one; realized that the Nazis had deployed themselves around our hide-out, waiting for me to make my move. Now they had me—and that message from Gollancz Dresca was in my pocket. If they ever got it away from me. . . .

I swerved, crammed the tiny sheet of tissue into my mouth, and swallowed it. Then I braced myself for the onslaught. I left-hooked the first Nazi, and his head bashed against the brickwork of the alley with a nasty sound that told of a split skull. The second one drew a Luger, aimed it at me. He pulled the trigger. A slug creased my ribs.

Before he could fire again, I grabbed the barrel of the automatic. I yanked it out of his fist. I bopped him with the butt; caught him full on the temple. I didn't even wait to see if I'd killed him. Instead, I pelted down the alley, gained the street, and took a chance. I walked forth from concealment.

Nobody tried to stop me. Maybe the two Prussians were the only ones detailed to the job; I don't know. But I didn't spot any more. And now I had only eight minutes to make my contact with Gollancz Dresca.

I didn't dare run, for fear of attracting attention. And there were no taxicabs in sight. So I set forth at a brisk walk. A tower clock in the old market-place was just booming out its twelfth somber stroke when I reached my destination.

A shadow moved in a doorway. "Kenthorne!"

It was Dresca, crouching there and trembling. He'd been through hell, and his nerve was gone. I clapped him on the shoulder and said: "Brace up. From now on, everything's okay." I handed him a flat packet. "Here's a phoney passport, a ticket to Paris, and a make-up kit. Remember how good you were at college theatricals in the old days? Very well; here's where your acting ability is going to save your neck. You'll disguise yourself as an old man—and make sure you resemble the photograph on this fake passport. After that, it should be easy sailing. I'll meet you in three days—at the Hotel Crillon, in Paris."

"Thanks, Jett!" he whispered brokenly. "I would have tried some such trick myself, but I couldn't get my hands on any make-up material. And it wouldn't have done me much good anyhow, without forged credentials to match. Now I'm all set." He hesitated. "What about Emy?"

"She's all right. I'll get her out of Prague somehow. She'll be with me when we meet in Paris. Now get busy." And I left him.

He scuttled off into the darkness. I turned back toward the house where I had left his sister waiting. The street was ominously quiet. I sneaked down the alley to the spot where I had conked the two Prussians.

I froze.

Only one of them lay there. The one with the smashed skull. His companion had vanished. That spelled trouble.

He must have revived from the gun-blow I'd dealt him. In which case he might have got in touch with Von Kragg and explained how I had escaped. Then Von Kragg might try to worm information out of Emy—

I LEAPED for the dangling rope of twisted sheets and blankets; went up hand-over-hand to the bedroom window. I peered over the sill. An oath tightened in my throat.

Emy was cowering despondently in a chair. Her gown had been ripped off, leaving her clad in nothing but sheer hose, brief panties, and a shimmering cascade of golden hair that streamed about her shoulders and veiled the rising hillocks of her breasts. Dull despair was in her eyes, and there was shame in the way she scrubbed at her lips with the back of her hand.

I heard Von Kragg snarling: "Since all this has not elicited information from you, perhaps there are other means of making you talk." He entwined his thick fingers in her hair; hauled her upright. He struck her with his fist. Not once, but several times. Struck her in the face, and on the body—

"You swine!" I roared. And I tumbled through the window; smashed myself at him.

I knew what he had been doing. And I realized that in spite of all his torture, Emy had refused to tell him what he wanted to know; had sacrificed herself in order to protect the brother she loved. . . .

Von Kragg released her when he heard my snarled challenge. He pivoted. His right hand dived for his holstered Mauser automatic.

I slugged him in the teeth; knocked him crashing against the wall. He landed with a jarring impact, but he had a jaw like cast iron. My punch had knocked him down, but it hadn't put him out. Up came his Mauser. His finger tightened on the trigger.

I swerved, even though I knew I'd be too late. Bullets aren't easily ducked. And yet his slug didn't get me. It spanked into the bureau mirror, shattered it. Flying fragments of glass rained through the room. Emy had saved my life. At the last instant she had hurled herself at Von Kragg's gun-hand, deflecting his aim.

He cursed her, gutturally. He came up on his knees; flung her away from him. She gasped as she caromed over a chair; doubled over, pressing her fingers to her waist. I said: "You woman-beating Hun!" and closed in on him.

I kicked at his right fist. His Mauser sailed out the window, and he bellowed with pain. Out in the corridor, hell had broken loose. Women were screaming, men cursing. Knuckles drummed on the door of the bedroom. I paid no attention to the uproar. I was locked against Von Kragg, and I intended to kill him. Kill him with my bare hands—for what he had made Emy suffer.

He tried to sink his teeth into my throat. I backed away; and I jabbed my thumbs into his blazing eyes. I did it deliberately. I wanted to blind him; to hurt him; to make him suffer the agonies of the damned before he died. He

(Continued on page 124)

By

HUGH SPEER

They told her that he was a wild beast, and she believed them. It hurt to have her numbered among his enemies—and yet, because she reminded him of a girl he once had loved, he did his best to save her

He slung the Frenchman bodily at Bowers, knocking the man over the rail. Then it was knives because knives are the weapons of the Islands.

RED EDEN

RED EDEN sailed his schooner into Pango Harbor, in the New Hebrides, loaded, packed, and jammed with copra. He was a hulk of a man, red-haired, red-bearded, and with a fuzz of red hair upon the great chest half-bare beneath the tattered sweater. Balancing himself drunkenly upon the heaving deck, he cursed his Kanaka seamen as they shortened sail. He had one arm about the black waist of a Melanesian girl, whose ideas of clothing were rudimentary, and the other about the print-clad form of a supple, seductive brown Polynesian lass.

This picture was a bad one from the moralist's point of view. Those two girls might not have looked right. Yet Eden's copra, bought at a forced price from intimidated coconut-growers in the remoter islands would probably have looked perfectly innocent. As a matter of fact, it was the other way about. That copra wasn't quite right; but everybody in the islands knew that Red Eden didn't often amuse himself with native girls. He had his arms about the two because he was a friendly soul, especially when he had filled up with liquor.

No, Eden was bringing the two girls to old Woo's trading-store on Pango because they had begged him to, and Eden didn't profess to be the guardian of anybody's morals. To be an inmate of Woo's place for a season meant money and gifts, thrills and excitement that would remain a cherished memory long after the girl had returned to her island home, to settle down as the mother of brown-skinned children, and a chewer of *kava.*

Red Eden was doing the girls a kindness, and he was embracing them in the exuberance of his happiness. Eden was going to Pango, where he could get drunk in company, and then he was going on to Sydney, with his load of copra bought and consigned, even if he had used high-handed methods to get it from the coconut-grower.

Who didn't trade that way in the remoter islands of the South Seas?

"You black-skinned sons of Satan, I'll tear you into little pieces!" roared Red Eden, as the schooner escaped the edge of the barrier reef by a marginal fraction, and glided on through the still water, toward the little wharf, the trading-store, and the native huts beneath the palm-trees.

There were other schooners in the harbor, and, beached not far away, was the burned out hulk of an Australian coastal vessel. The blackened hull had been almost totally consumed by fire, the superstructure was a charred and twisted mass. Red Eden studied it as he glided in to anchorage. He hadn't heard about the wreck—but then he had been in the remoter islands, picking up copra.

THE traders had come to Pango, which was the center for many illicit activities that could not be carried on in islands with French and British consulates. Pango was the place where stolen pearls were negotiated; Australian firms of the highest reputation made deals for copra there. Guileless natives were still brought there to be "blackbirded" for Queensland plantations.

Red Eden stepped onto the wharf and sniffed the odor of dead fish and rotting oysters, and his heart was uplifted. He saw the reeling traders passing in and out of old Woo's store, the grinning girls coming out in Woo's store-finery. This was the old life; this was the life he had known for a dozen years. Sometimes Red Eden recalled the days when he had been a mild young theological student in a New England seminary. Years ago—and what a laugh, what a laugh if anybody had known!

"Hey, Red!"

"Back agen, Red? The old place ain't the same without you! Let's get a drink!"

The crowd of drunken, reeling traders was all about him. Red Eden staggered into the store. "Here's two girls I brought you from Opago Island," he told the bespectacled old Chinese proprietor. "They was crazy to come. But see they're treated right, because they're friends of mine."

Woo grinned, and set out a bottle of squareface on his counter, which was piled high with feminine fripperies. With squeals of delight, Eden's two friends assailed them. A little crowd of hard-faced men had gathered about them, appraising them. The frizzy-haired Melanesian had only the advantage of extreme youth; she was about fifteen, and her little breasts were budding out of her chest. Good enough for some, maybe; but the brown Polynesian was a lithe, splendid creature, and she had a circle of men about her already.

"What you brought, Red—copra?" asked a shrewd little dealer from Sydney.

"I'll talk business when I get damn' well ready," said Eden. "What's this coming?"

A YOUNG fellow in the tattered remnants of a suit of ducks, with a panama perched over one ear, was entering the store. He looked about twenty years of age. His face was rather vacuous, and he was very evidently English. He was quite drunk, and he rolled up aggressively to the counter.

"Chalk me up another whiskey, Woo," he drawled—and then Red Eden knew that he was English.

"What the hell have we got here?" asked Eden.

"English Honorable. Younger son of a lord. Name Freddy Greer. One of the two persons saved from the wreck last month."

"I saw her hulk, coming in," said Eden. He put his hand on Freddy's shoulder. "You're drinking with me," he said.

Freddy Greer turned aggressively. "I don't drink with riffraff," he shouted, and flung the contents of his glass into Red's face.

Then everybody held his breath. Tempers were short in the Islands, and nobody had ever insulted Red Eden before. And Red's great hands could have torn the young fellow to pieces. But Red stood motionless, with the liquor dropping off his cheeks.

"Come away, Freddy," said a trader, catching Freddy by the arm.

"I'm *having* another drink. Chalk me up another, Woo. I'll settle with you when the next ship comes in."

Woo poured the drink, and Freddy drank. He walked away from the counter, through the crowd of copra-dealers and pearl-thieves.

"How do the blooming Limies get away with that sort of thing?" somebody asked.

But they were all looking at Red. The drops of liquor were still trickling down from Red's cheeks and forehead, but Red was grinning.

"How about that wreck?" he asked.

"Honorable Freddy and Miss Beth was the only two passengers to be rescued when the *Olympia* burned. She went up like a torch. Freddy was going to Brisbane. Remittance-man. We thought his dad was good for money, but the old man turned him down. Woo read the letter. Freddy don't know yet."

"What about the girl?"

"Daughter of old John Tyson, the missionary, who died on Oswago Island two months ago. She was going home to England."

"Where are they living?" asked Red Eden.

"We've given Freddy a hut. Beth Tyson's been sick—nearly died. Pneumonia, it looked like. She's being took care of by Woo's Number One wife back there."

He pointed behind the store, and Red Eden swayed through the crowd, which opened to let him pass.

ANDERSON, the little Sydney trader, was talking with the only two other sober men in Woo's place. One of them said, "Red's schooner's crammed with A1 quality copra. He made that poor Dutchman on Brantovo Island sell him his crop for a song."

"I heard so," said Anderson.

"You buying?" queried the other.

The little trader grinned. "Not unless I have to, Lucas. But it's difficult to cross Red Eden."

"Red's ruled this roost too long," said Marais, a black-bearded Frenchman. "That copra's worth a sizable sum. And that girl—" He licked his lips.

They put their heads together, whispering. The crowd in Woo's place was watching them without hearing the conversation. They guessed the tenor of it, nevertheless. Red Eden had ruled the roost too long. And Freddy Greer was a washout. Everybody knew that Woo's wire to Baron Greer had elicited a complete repudiation of Freddy's appeal for funds. Freddy didn't know it, because Woo hadn't shown him the letter.

And Beth Tyson was homeless and friendless. There wasn't a man there who wouldn't have slit Marais' throat for Beth. She was recovering from pneumonia now in the back of Woo's store. Marais was the big man on Pango, but nobody had ever tried to cross Red Eden. The crowd was wondering how the situation would crystallize, with the drunken young fool, Freddy Greer, and the convalescent girl.

They licked their lips and drank, and watched Marais and Anderson and Lucas, and guessed that Red Eden would shortly meet an unprofitable end.

RED EDEN strode through the hanging curtains back of Woo's store. A little Chinese girl in filmy trousers squealed and dodged out of his way. A gaunt old Chinese woman, also in trousers, but thick duck trousers, tried to bar Eden's entrance. Eden strode on into the room where Beth Tyson was sitting in a steamer chair.

She was wearing silk pajamas that revealed all the beauty of her form. Breasts danced beneath the filmy covering as she started up in alarm. The superb arch of the hips, and the little bare feet beneath the trouser legs, thrust into straw slippers. Freddy was standing beside her.

"What do you want?" cried the girl.

Red Eden didn't know. He was too drunk to know. He stood staring at Beth, and swaying. Perhaps deep in his mind was the idea of taking Beth away on his schooner, with the copra. He knew what her fate would be among the wild beasts of Pango Island. But he only stood swaying and mumbling, and remembering the girl who had looked like Beth, and for whose sake he had given up being a theological student years before. Then Freddy came reeling toward him, his fists whirling.

"Get the hell out of here!" he shouted, adding a string of foul expletives.

The Limy was a spunky little devil. This time he struck Eden in the face, and it was like a slap from

He forced her into a seat in the dinghy though she screamed for help.

a girl. One blow of Eden's would have smashed the Limy to the floor. But again Eden didn't strike. He stood swaying, and looking at the girl, on her feet now, pulling the trousers of her pajamas higher over an inch of delicious whiteness, her face frantic with terror.

"I didn't come to hurt you," Eden mumbled.

And he thought again of the time when he had been a theological student, years before. He had studied Greek and Hebrew—he, the toughest roughneck in the islands. It was a joke, being a man. Ten years of trading in the New Hebrides had remoulded him. He had drunk the strong wine of life. Fighting, trading, drinking, love affairs — but never with native women, except the little Polynesian girl years ago, and Marya, three years ago, and the girl who had saved him in a nasty jam on one of the Loyalties. That wasn't many. But why was Red Eden thinking all this?

He knew the reason as he looked at Beth and saw the tremulous movements of her breast beneath the pajama coat. It was twelve years since Red Eden had seen a white woman who had the power to do what Beth Tyson was doing to him now.

"I came in to say—I'm your friend. Look out for those fellows," mumbled Eden.

Freddy snarled and made at him again. Poor kids! Red Eden turned and went away. He had a vague consciousness of the gaunt Chinese woman standing before him, waving him in the right direction. Then he weaved his way to the guest-rooms behind Woo's store. He found one, and dropped upon the bed. He didn't even lay his revolver beside his hand. Consciousness was blotted out instantly.

MARAIS and Lucas were in the room with Freddy and Beth, who now had a blanket draped about her pajama-clad form.

"He's dead drunk now, but he'll wake up by nightfall," Lucas explained. "We've got to do it quick."

"Do what?"

"There's no law, no Government on Pango Island. We're thinking of you, Miss Beth. Red Eden's ruled this roost too long. We're going to try him by a special court, and maroon him on one of the lesser islands, where he won't bother nobody again."

"That's the idea!" cried Freddy

"We've got to get rid of a wild beast, Miss Beth. Then we'll take you and Mr. Greer to Sydney on his schooner and report to the authorities, though this is French territory, and we don't have to. We want to do things proper and legal."

He was looking at the white curve of Beth's shoulder above the blanket. Marais' face was bestial. Beth could see that. Fear and doubt were struggling within her, and she looked desperately at Freddy Greer for guidance.

"You're going to arrest him now?" whispered the girl.

"We've got to. You and Greer keep quiet. He's as drunk as a log, the Chink girl says."

They left the room. Beth turned to Freddy. "Do you trust them?" she asked. "I feel—I feel somehow as if that man Eden was better than all of them."

"He's a wild beast. God, Beth, we've got to get off this island! We'll be married in Sydney, and if dad's sent me the five hundred pounds I asked for, to this place, I'll stop the check. Everything will be all right."

"I don't trust Lucas and Marais." She shivered. Instinct told her what fate she might expect when they had settled with Eden. She leaned back helplessly against Freddy, and he put his arm about her and tried to comfort her, while they both listened for the expected sounds of fight.

Beth had met Freddy aboard the ill-fated *Olympia,* and their romance had been sweet. But would he measure up to what a woman expected of a man? He had gone to pieces during their brief stay on Pango Island, drinking all the time. And Beth suspected there had been a native girl. But she didn't like to think of that. Still, one can't be the daughter of a missionary on one of the outer islands without getting a very realistic understanding of men.

Beth waited, shuddering—and then it came. A sound like that of a wild beast springing upon its prey. The crack of a gun. Yells everywhere about Woo's store, and screams of Chinese wives and Polynesian girls.

BETH sprang to her feet and rushed from the room, pushing away Freddy, who tried to detain her. In the guest room, Eden was struggling with a mass of men. The blood was running down his cheek, where Lucas' bullet had grazed it, but Lucas was lying insensible upon the floor, stunned by one blow from one of Eden's mighty fists.

A dozen of the riffraff of the island, petty traders who wanted a chance at Eden's copra, were circling around, knives in their hands —the favorite weapon of the islands. Marais was crouching in one corner, his own knife drawn, watching for the chance to take Eden from behind.

Just as Beth reached the room, Eden bellowed again. He hurled his massive body against his assailants, and his fists swung and sent them crashing to the floor. And at the same moment Marais sprang, his white teeth gleaming above his black beard.

Beth leaped forward with a scream, and caught the Frenchman's arm. The blow of the knife, deflected, inflicted a slight wound upon her shoulder, from which a little trickle of blood began to drip.

The blanket had fallen from her shoulders, the pajama coat had come unfastened, and the sight of the small, oscillating breasts, with the trickle of red blood between them, drove Marais to a pitch of madness. For this was a white woman, such as was hardly ever seen on Pango, and the whiteness and the softness of her made Marais a fighting beast.

With a shriek, he thrust the girl from him, and sprang at Eden, slashing a vicious uppercut with his knife. Some demoniac guardian must have guided Eden then. Still reeling drunk, roaring and laughing, he lashed out a terrific blow that struck the knife and sent it flying out of the Frenchman's hand, and then he went on and caught

Marais in the midriff, doubling him up in agony.

"Come on, you lice!" bawled Eden.

But his assailants had fled, and he was standing in the room with Beth and Freddy, with the two unconscious men upon the floor.

"You can't scare me!" Freddy shouted.

Eden struck him for the first time. It was a blow of his forearm, delivered across the cheek, and it inflicted no bruise, but it hurled Freddy Greer across the room, upon the prostrate body of Lucas.

Beth shrieked, and sprang at Eden like a wildcat. Eden caught the girl up in his arms, and again that gargantuan laugh of his boomed out. This was living—this was the life he had chosen!

HE HELD the girl, kicking and struggling, and he felt the warmth of her bosom against him, but it didn't stir him—not as it would have stirred most men. For this girl seemed to bring back memories of the life he had long ago forsaken, and of the woman who had looked like her but wasn't she.

Sometimes, when he was sober, Eden had dreamed of leaving the life of the islands behind him, and finding haven in his own country—with a woman like Beth. Then, when he was drunk, he had cursed himself for a fool, because he hadn't seen that sort of woman in his twelve years of trading.

And always his earnings went at the Sydney gambling-tables, or on things he would have been ashamed to have had known—such as helping poor devils who had lost their ships, and had never repaid him for staking them to a share in another schooner. Money had always slipped through Eden's fingers like water.

His mind was a medley of all these memories as he carried Beth, clawing and scratching and kicking. He shifted her higher in his arms, and felt the smooth skin of her warm against his face. "You damn' little fool!" he cried in the girl's ear. "If ever you hope to get away from Pango, now's your chance!"

"You let me go! You've killed Freddy!"

She didn't understand, and there was no way of making her understand. But the liquor was clearing out of Eden's head now. He knew his only chance lay in the fact that the traders were not united. They all wanted a chance at his load of copra, but they weren't all going to fight for Marais and Lucas.

Red Eden stumbled through the doorway, holding the kicking, struggling girl high in his arms. Again the little Chinese girl in the filmy trousers scuttled out of Eden's way. Two figures leaped at him with flashing knives. One was a half-caste, Nigger Jake. Red Eden flung the girl behind him, dodged Jake, and knocked him senseless. He twisted the other's knife-arm until he heard the bone crack like a pistol-shot, then flung the screaming man away.

He picked up Beth, still yelling and clawing, and staggered on into Woo's trading-store. There was a frenzied scuttling out through the doorway. Eden passed through. It was almost dark now, and the large swinging oil lamp had been lit, but the store was emptied in a moment.

AGAIN he shifted Beth higher, and struggled on down the coral walk toward the wharf where his dinghy lay. Two figures appeared:

"Master! Master!"

With the native girl in the circle of his arm, he struck Beth and sent her reeling.

They were Bembo and George, Eden's two Kanakas. They had long knives in their hands, and they gaped and grinned.

"Back to the ship! We're sailing!"

"No sail till the tide cross reef in the morning, master," said Bembo.

Eden cursed. He had forgotten that. He carried Beth to the dinghy and forced her into a seat. She was screaming for help. Among the palms shadowy figures were massing. A rush might come at any moment. Eden drew his gun. There began an aimless shooting from the palms, but it was impossible to aim at the shadowy dinghy and its occupants in the darkness. Eden held Beth in her place, while Bembo cast off the rope. George leaped in and took the oars, and Bembo followed.

"Freddy, Freddy—help!" wailed Beth.

Eden shook her until she subsided, sobbing. She began struggling again, however, when Eden carried her up the ladder, and more fiercely when he carried her below. He flung her down upon the bunk in the tiny cabin.

"You're a fool. You don't know what those men would have done to you. I was trying to get you away," said Eden, looking at her and wondering how a girl so desirable could have the mind of a child.

"Freddy's dead. We were engaged to be married. And I don't trust you."

Eden took a long swill from a bottle upon the table. His eyes fell upon a suit of dungarees, hanging upon a wall.

"Get into those!" he commanded.

"I won't!"

Eden caught at the filmy pajama coat and ripped it from top to bottom. Beth gasped and tried to cover her bosom with her hands. The sight of the girl's rounded breasts began to arouse new emotions in Eden.

"Get into those, or I'll put them on you myself!" he shouted. "Going to do what I say!"

"Ye—yes, if you'll get out of here."

RED EDEN took another swig at the bottle, and went up the companion to the deck. He didn't quite know what he was going to do with Beth, but a little fool like that didn't deserve—God, didn't deserve to be counted with the few memories he cherished! He would have liked to have saved Freddy, too. But it wasn't likely that Marais and his crowd would do anything very bad to Freddy. His old man would come across with plenty of money, sooner or later.

Eden had a bow-gun, firing a small-calibre shell, but that wasn't any use on a dark night. That was only useful for holding off pursuers who wanted Eden's copra, or had come to the conclusion that it was their own. In the tiny lazaret next to the wheel-house Eden had three rifles and half-a-dozen revolvers. He broke out two revolvers and handed them to George and Bembo, with a handful of cartridges apiece.

"If they try to board us, make plenty dead mans," said Eden, and the Kanakas grinned. Eden guessed that they would use their knives, though.

Six hours to wait before the tide would lift the schooner over the bar. The night was as black as sin, no moon, and the heavens overcast with clouds. Eden knew his copra was worth big money. The question was how many men Marais and Lucas could get to follow them. Eden was certain that an attack was coming.

He had locked Beth into the cabin. Once or twice he heard her hammering with her fists, but he paid no attention. He knew she couldn't break down the door. And she couldn't get out of the porthole. Eden's schooner didn't have that kind of porthole. He waited on deck with George and Bembo.

LUCAS, with a lump the size of an egg upon his forehead, and Marais, still stiff from Eden's blow in the midriff, were putting their heads together with several more.

"She can't get over the reef till dawn," said Lucas, "and there's only three of them. The night's as black as pitch, and there won't be no moon for hours. I'm going to get that—. Besides, he stole that copra from that poor Dutchman on Brantovo Island. We'll divide up the copra, and—"

"You've got to see that Beth's rescued," said Freddy. He wasn't drunk now—white-faced and fearful. "God, she's been in that beast's power for hours. By morning—"

The others laughed uncomfortably. Marais said, "That's the chief reason why we've got to get Eden. If he slips away, he'll take her to one of them haunts of his in the outer islands."

"God!" said Freddy, shuddering.

Lucas grinned at Marais. The two men had come to a perfect understanding. It oughtn't to be a difficult matter to capture the schooner. There would be seven of them, all told — Lucas, Marais, Freddy, old Bowers, Fish, and Nigger Jake. There would be a fair split between Lucas, Marais, and the little Sydney trader—because they meant to get rid of Nigger Jake, Bowers, and Fish. As for Freddy, they'd sail the schooner into Sydney harbor and keep him under lock and key somewhere, until his old man decided to pay up.

As for Beth, the three of them would just cruise until they were tired of Beth. There were plenty of secluded islands along the Great Barrier Reef, which would be just right for that sort of expedition.

"You swear, whatever happens, you'll do your best for Beth?" asked white-faced Freddy.

"Sure we will. Have another drink, son," said Lucas, patting him on the shoulder.

"I'll kill that devil!" shouted Freddy, a little later, as the liquor began to revive him.

"I'm going to ask five thousand pounds for Freddy's ransom," said Lucas to Marais.

"I'd double it."

"Maybe. Anyway, there's going to be more in it than a load of copra."

IT WAS well after midnight when the two dinghies put off from the shore. Marais was in one of

(Continued on page 103)

Invitation to

By WILLIAM B. RAINEY

The finger was tight on the trigger and the muzzle pointed at his heart.

CHARLES LANE'S slave brought him the letter. "One 'uf dese French niggers give it to me," Horsehair said, "an' wuz gone fore Ah could say, 'Hit's er hot day, ain't it, an' how do you do?' She jes' give it me, an' went." He sighed heavily. "An' she wuz sho' a sweet thing uf light brown."

Lane read the letter in the flagged courtyard, sipping his brandy, his lace collar open against the heat.

It was written in French, in dark ink, upon heavy, perfumed paper. It read:

ROMANCE

A strange woman asked Lane to hold some compromising letters for her. And then she led him to a rendezvous that jeopardized his very life! He wanted to help her yet she seemed to be plotting his death!

You must forgive me, but desperation forces me to write to you. I do not think you have ever seen me, but I have seen you, monsieur, and I have heard of you as a brave and gallant gentleman—and one always ready to interest himself in a young lady's behalf. I wonder if this is true, because I am in great need of someone's help.

Janice.

There was no address, no name except that single word.

"A nice handwriting," Lane said, his left eyebrow faintly higher than the right. He passed the paper close under his nose. "And a costly and excellent perfume. She might be a lady it would be pleasant to interest myself in. Didn't the slave give you an address, Horsehair?"

"She ain't gimme nothin' but de note and de go-by," Horsehair said.

"You had never seen her before? You don't know whom she belongs to?"

"Ah never seen her befo', but Ah aims to interest myself in seein' her again," Horsehair said. "Ah got er feelin' Ah'm the boy to make dat gal happy."

"Maybe she'll be looking you up later."

"Ah won't be hard to find," Horsehair said. "Not fer dat light-brown sho nuff piece of love-on-de-hoof."

But Charles Lane heard no more that night, nor the next day nor the next night. He shrugged his shoulders and forgot the letter.

TOWARD twilight of the second day, when Horsehair returned with a large basket from the wine merchant, he had news. "Ah seen her!" he said. "An' dat gal got more curves dan de Mississippi ribber. Dese French niggers got class!"

"I don't care how the slave girl looks," Lane said. "Did she have another letter for me?"

"Naw, sur."

"What did she say?"

Horsehair looked dismal. "Twan't nothin' to 'mount to nothin'," he said. "She ast me, 'What yo' marster think uf dat letter?' An' I say, 'He ast me whar you and whar yo' mistress, and how's Ah to tell him?' And she say, "Yo' marster lak pretty womens?' And I say, 'Do Ah look like a nigger belong to a damn' fool?' And den Ah ast her whars de place she rests her shoes come night, and she say ain't none uf my no-mind, and flounces off. Dat gal is trouble to reach!"

IT WAS the next evening that the box arrived, a small but heavy box that the slave girl could scarcely carry. She had stepped out of the deep shadows to give the box to Horsehair and whisper, "For your marster," and then she was gone again with Horsehair shouting futilely after her.

There was a note accompanying the box. It read:

Again I must beg your help and your forgiveness for having asked it.

Will you keep this box until I call for it? The box contains letters which I was foolish enough to write, and which now I am in terrible fear of losing to a man who would use them against me. I cannot explain more fully now, though I promise to do so later. I am placing myself completely in your hands by trusting these to you, but I do so with absolute faith.

Janice.

"So-o," Lane said, waving the letter gently beneath his nose. "A lady who writes compromising letters, and who uses my favorite of all perfumes." He lifted one end of the box, and lifting it made the muscles pull taut within his arm. "Letters?" he said musingly. "They must be written in words of gold to weigh this much." But he placed the box unopened within his bedroom. The lady had promised to call for it. Perhaps things were moving toward a climax.

The third letter arrived exactly a week after the first one. And Charles Lane felt his pulse beat faster as he read. It named an hour and a place for a meeting.

And yet I have no right to ask that you should come. There are men who will kill to stop the thing I must do. In asking you to help me I am asking you to risk your life for a girl whom you have never seen, but whose cause is a right and just one. And if we are successful, any reward I am able to give will be yours for the asking.

Janice.

Charles Lane considered the letter for a space of seconds, one straight, dark eyebrow minutely higher than the other. "There are those," he thought, "who might not consider this the wisest thing to do; but it certainly gives promise of being the most interesting. And the man who tries to use wisdom in dealing with women," he decided, "is a damn' fool."

So that shortly before midnight the two horses slushed through the mud of New Orleans' narrow and foul-smelling streets. Lane rode in front, muffled in a thin summer cloak of dark blue. There were two pistols in the sash about his waist, and his rapier struck faint chimes within its scabbard of handworked silver. Horsehair brought up the rear. He needed no dark cloak, because against the night only the whites of his eyes (and his teeth, when he grinned) were visible.

The place where Lane halted was a half block from Madam Brovard's saloon. A bit of yellow light came through the saloon windows, and occasionally there was the sound of loud voices, or the ringing laughter of one of the girls who waited on Madam Brovard's tables, when they were not otherwise employed. In the other direction a single oil streetlamp made a splotch of smoky color. No other light was visible.

He had been there ten minutes when he heard the carriage.

THE horses' hoofs made sucking noises in the mud, mingled with the sound of the turning wheels. Then he could see the carriage as a shapeless blot against the night. It stopped a few feet from where Lane waited, and he spurred his horse forward.

He could scarcely see the girl's face against the carriage window.

Her voice was a tense, frightened whisper. "Monsieur Lane?"

"Mademoiselle Janice?"

"Yes. Who is that with you?"

"A slave."

"Let him take your horse home. Come in the carriage—with me."

"Yes, mademoiselle." He swung from the stirrup to the carriage step. The girl had opened the door for him. He sat beside her in the darkness.

He could smell the perfume that she used, heavy upon the warm darkness. He could tell that she wore a white, low cut gown and that above it her shoulders were bare and cream-colored in the gloom. Then they were passing Madam Brovard's saloon and for an instant pale light swam over them. Charles Lane took a deep breath. He was a man who appreciated beautiful women.

The girl's hair was black and shimmering as the leaves of a magnolia seen by moonlight. Her face was small, oval, with widely set black eyes and a full, crimson mouth that looked moist and hungry for kissing. The dress left the upper slopes of her breasts bare—full, firm, and white as the fabric that partially covered them.

The carriage rounded a corner. The turn made the girl sway so that her shoulder touched Lane. When the carriage was rolling straight again, she did not move except to tilt her face up toward him.

"You were very brave to come," she said.

"If I had known how beautiful you are, I'd have been there hours ago."

She smiled. In the darkness he could see the white, even line of her teeth. "I have been told that you were very gallant—not at all the sort of man that we in Louisiana have always considered the Yankees to be."

"Thank you," Lane said. "Any South Carolinian would consider that a compliment."

The carriage rounded another corner, making Lane sway toward the girl this time, and it seemed almost accidental that his arm went around her. The flesh of her shoulder was like warm and yielding satin beneath his fingers. A smoky street light glistened for a moment on the soft curves of her breast, on her face with the full, damp mouth lifted toward him. He could feel his blood moving faster through his veins. His arm tightened around her. She made no move to pull free.

"Where are we going?" he asked huskily.

She whispered, "To a place I know. Where we will be safe, and alone."

"Alone? This mission you wanted me to help with . . . .?"

"When we get there. It is only a short distance now." She was quiet for a long moment, looking up at him. "Until then. . . ." she whispered. One arm slid up around his shoulders.

He was kissing her, fiercely, the two of them clinging together, their bodies pressed hard together, her breasts warm against him. He could feel the long, quivering tremors that ran through her. Her hands trembled eagerly against his shoulders and face.

He figured that whatever it was

Once again he thought he recognized something familiar in that elusive perfume.

she wanted him to do, he was already getting his reward.

And then he stopped figuring altogether . . . until, "Here's the place," she said.

IT WAS a small, dark house with tight-shuttered windows, and though he had been too occupied to pay close attention to their direction he guessed it to be somewhere near Rampart Street, in the section where many of the town's most elegant gentlemen housed their octoroon sweethearts.

The carriage rolled into a small, high-walled courtyard, and the slave opened the door. There was the odor of wisteria here, heady upon the still heat of the night. Charles Lane followed the girl across the dark courtyard. He heard the click of her key in the lock; a door opened and she stepped through into utter darkness. Her voice came back to him, "Come in. I will find candles in a moment."

He was stepping over the sill when some lack of weight, something that he felt without realizing, caused him to put one hand against his waist. He realized suddenly, violently, that his pistols were gone! And he was spinning sideways at the same moment that the knife slashed downward from out the darkness. The blade ripped his cloak, tangled it as he spun, and fell with a clatter of steel upon the floor.

Inside the room the girl cried once.

A second body struck against Lane, staggered him. A man yelled hoarsely, "Lights!" Lane sensed more than saw the upraised arm, the knife. Leaping backward he flung up his own left arm and pain slashed thin across it. Then his rapier lashed free. There was the ring of steel on steel, and he drove the point at that blacker spot in the darknes, felt the sliding grip on the blade as it plunged into flesh. In the darkness the man's cry was choked and horrible. His body made a dull thud when it fell.

From near the doorway a tongue of flame leaped out and the room shook with the roar of a pistol. Then the black rectangle of the doorway was made blacker as a body dived through it and vanished into the night. Lane jumped after the man, but he didn't know exactly where the other one had fallen, for he stumbled over him (must have stepped on the man's face from the feel of it) and fell headlong. He rolled and was on his feet again and running.

In the courtyard he stopped, hearing the sound of a horse in full gallop.

He turned toward the carriage, saying, "Did you see that man? Where was his horse hidden?" But there was no answer. The slave who had driven the carriage was gone. The two pistols were there, however, pushed down behind the seat, and he got them and thrust them into his sash. The naked rapier still in his hand, he went toward the house again. The open doorway now was bright yellow with light.

The girl stood in the middle of the floor holding a candelabra in which five candles sputtered and burned. Her face was bloodless, only her mouth showing crimson against her drawn cheeks. The throat of her dress, low to begin with, was torn so that he could see the shadowed valley between her trembling breasts.

ON THE floor a man lay with eyes wide open and hands pressed tight against his stomach and with blood sliding quiet and dark between his fingers. The man shuddered and died, and lay there with his eyes still open and his hands still pressed against his stomach.

"They were here," the girl said in a voice of dazed amazement. "They were waiting for us when we came!"

"So it seems," Lane said. He closed the door behind him, then crossed the room toward the girl who had put the candelabra upon a table. She was staring at the body upon the floor.

"'You killed one of them!" she whispered.

"It does look that way, doesn't it." He was close to her, looking quizzically at her with one eyebrow slightly lifted; but there was something ruthless about the set of his mouth now, and muscles made cords along his jaw. "Suppose you tell me what this is all about?"

The girl put both hands upon his chest, her oval face tilted up toward him. Her dark hair had come loose and hung thick about her throat and shoulders. Her breathing made the rounded bosom move gently. "I warned you it would be dangerous. But I didn't think they would be here. I didn't think they knew about this place."

"Who are they?"

"My two uncles." Her eyes lowered, then raised to his again. "I am their ward, but the jewels, the gold, even the property is legally mine. They have kept me shut up in what should be my own home. They have even tried to force me to marry one of my uncles—the one there on the floor. And I had no one I could go to. No one knows now whether Louisiana belongs to France or Spain or to the American colonies, and what little law there is in this city will not dare trouble my uncles. And so I came to you."

"To do what?"

"There is a ship sailing tomorrow for New York. If I could get on it, away from my uncles, carrying some wealth with me. . . . I have the money hidden here. But you must help me get it, and get on the ship."

Lane's left eyebrow was still twitched high on his forehead. "Why didn't these uncles simply kill you and be done with it?"

"When I am dead, the property goes to the Church. The Church is the only thing in Louisiána strong enough to defeat my uncles. So they must keep me alive." She came very close to him now, pressing herself against him, her lips moist and full below his. She whispered, "We will be safe here—until morning. . . ."

He put his left arm around her. The sword still was in his right hand. He kissed her and she began to tremble against him. "Ah-h," Lane sighed, "I wish that you were telling the truth, because we could pass the time very pleasantly. But I must forego immediate pleasure for the sake of living longer."

"We will be safe here."

(Continued on page 110)

Out of the Alhambra came a rush of Palace guards.

THE LAUGHING MOOR

He escaped death—only to become a galley slave. And from there his trail of adventure led to Moorish Spain, and to the citadel imprisoning the lovely Zorayah. Who would have suspected the brave captain of the Granada Guard, disappointed in love and with a bitter laugh on his lips, of being a fugitive from England?

A Novelette
by LEW MERRILL

YOUNG FRANCIS BLOUNT opened his eyes and realized that he was still alive. That amazing fact made him oblivious of the throbbing pain in his temple. He groaned, and wriggled across a dead man who lay skewered beside him, and then he remembered that he had seen Richard Crookback, of England, fall fighting that day, and that the cause of the White Rose, which Francis's family had served, was dead forever.

He found a sword hidden under a corspe, a good damascened sword of Moorish steel. He drew his arms more tightly into the body of his doublet. It was cold, that night of August 22, in the year 1485, but the dead slept colder under the drizzling rain. Francis turned his face westward toward the Welsh marches. That was his country.

Baron Eastover, his lord, would protect him. And there was the dark beauty of the Lady Alayne,

his daughter. Francis's small patrimony had prevented his aspiring to her hand, but, before Francis rode off to fight for Crookback, Alayne had plucked a rose—a white rose—from a trellis, and placed it in a slit of his doublet.

Francis strode like a madman heedless of the distance, gulping ale at inns and snatching up bread, and none of the rabble of disbanded soldiers whom he encountered dared to cross him. So, three days later, he saw the towers and battlements of Eastover Castle before him. In the twilight he made his way to the close behind the castle. It was enclosed by yew and hawthorn hedges, and roses rioted gaily over them.

Alayne was pacing the close with her brother, Sir Philip, a young sprig in slashed doublet and red shoes with upcurving tips.

Francis didn't realize that his doublet was rent and muddied, and his trunk-hose discolored with ditch-water, nor that one side of his face was a mass of congealed blood from the cross-bow bolt that had grazed his head. Nor that he looked like a madman as he stood there, clutching his drawn sword.

Alayne saw him, and cried out sharply.

"Aye, it is Francis Blount. I saw King Richard die at Bosworth. I have—come home."

And he plucked a white rose from a trellis and thrust it into his garment. Sir Philip sidled away.

"Throw that away! Do you not know that the white rose is the sign of death in England?" Alayne cried. "How did you dare come back?"

"Why, to see you," answered Francis.

"You must flee at once and never see me again—do you understand? You fool, do you not know that your name is one of the foremost on the list of the proscribed, because of your family's loyalty to the White Rose? Within a few minutes my brother Philip will be back with the men-at-arms."

Francis stepped to the trellis and tore the climbing roses from their supports, and left them lying, a trail of white in the gloaming.

"I go, then. I see it is true, that women know neither faith nor loyalty. But some day I shall come back for you."

He caught her in his arms, and felt the pressure of her small, firm breasts against him, the warmth and softness of her. For a moment she lay passive in his arms, and their lips met. Then she tore herself away and struck at him.

Francis released her with a laugh, and strode into the murk of the August evening, just as an outcry sounded from the battlements.

CHAPTER II

"My Son! My Son!"

SINCE boyhood Francis had loved Deeside Port, whose waters have long since been silted up, whose houses have disappeared beneath them. Deeside Port was doing a roaring business that night, for the ships from Burgundy, the Low Countries, the Spains, Portugal, and Moorish Granada, which had brought the new King of England, Henry

Tudor, and his troops, were tied up at the wharves. Henry Tudor had overthrown Richard Crookback, and he had paid his transport. Seamen were brawling and swaggering in the streets. Deeside Port was reaping a rich harvest of moidores and crowns.

Here was a great Genoese galleass, with her three masts and twenty guns. Here were the slim oared galleys of Barbary and Granada. In the taverns, Moors who had forgotten the Prophet's law against liquor shouted tipsily with Burgundians and Venetians.

Francis walked down the street like a man in a dream. His mother's great diamond had slipped from his finger in the fight at Bosworth. "Now, had I that, I could take passage for any port in the world," he thought.

One of the good citizens passed him, recognized him, and cried his name.

"Silence, fool!" hissed Francis, holding sword-point to the man's breast. But a dozen voices took up the cry, and a mob came swarming forward.

"Death to the traitor!"

"Nay, there is blood-money on his head. Take him alive!"

They rushed at Francis with axe and crowbar. Francis swung his sword, pierced one man through the belly, and clove a circle around him, glaring into the faces of the townsmen.

There came a rush along the street, and Francis saw the fierce, bearded faces of a band of Moorish sailors. "Allah! Allah!" he shouted—which was the only Arabic he knew.

YELLING in answer, the Moors flung themselves upon the men of Deeside Port. A scurry of knife-thrusts opened the way. Francis's rescuers stared at him, and then there rang out a burst of stentorian laughter.

For this fair-haired young man in the tattered doublet might be a Castilian, but he couldn't possibly be a Moor. Why, his face, stubbly though it was, had recently been shaven!

Somebody yelled, and Francis's rescuers began dragging him toward a wharf, where a red lateen sail was beginning to ascend the foremast of a galley. But the townsmen were not done. Blood-money was blood-money. Crowbar smashed skull, knives slipped between ribs. Mauled by both sides, Francis was knocked down and dragged through the mire toward the galley.

Below, in a frightful stench, Francis found himself among some threescore wretches seated on either side of a long central gangway, manning the oars.

A negro was on one side of him, a Ventian or Genoese on the other. A chain was shackled about his waist. A drum began to beat with accelerating tempo. The great handle of the oar leaped toward Francis's face. He had to grip it or be brained—and next moment all the oars were sweeping mechanically through the water.

Now Francis understood what had happened to him. A galley-slave was the small currency of the sea. But his newborn hatred of England lent him tireless strength. Sometimes he heard himself laughing as he pulled at the oar. He saw one of the bos'ns on the central gangway pointing him out to a slim young Moor, and, later, to an old man with a white beard falling to his waist. The old Moor pinched Francis's arm muscles.

FRANCIS became a favorite of the bos'ns. It was a long time since a slave, so young and vigorous, had been put to the oar. He dropped exhausted, and awoke when the wine-steeped bread was thrust into his mouth. Night and day became equally meaningless to him. Several times he was aware of the old, white-bearded Moor standing on the gangway, looking at him. But he didn't know that the Moor was estimating his value in the *sokh,* the slave-market.

One evening Francis, awaking, felt the whip for the first time. "Row, Christian swine!" the bos'n yelled.

For an instant Francis strained in fury against his chain—then the oar came forward, and he was compelled to grasp it. The slaves pulled madly, and, as the galley came about, there sounded the roar of a gun, and a culverin-ball mowed its way amidships, decapitating two of the oarsmen as it passed out on

He watched the corpse roll down the rocks to the Vega.

the other side of the galley.

Yells sounded from the outer darkness, and were answered by the Moors, massing on the high poop and bow.

Then the iron-beaked prow of a hostile galley sheared off a dozen oars as it careened alongside. The huge handle of Francis's oar brained the man beside him, and thudded past within a few inches of his face. Overhead Francis could hear the yells of the combatants as they thudded to and fro upon the deck.

Suddenly Francis laughed, and, with a mighty heave of his strong young body, he tore himself free of bench and chain, and raced along the gangway. A guard ran at him with a scimitar. Francis sprang like a tiger, and guard and scimitar went clattering down. Francis picked up the weapon and ran up on deck.

The assailants of the galley were pale-faced men—probably pirates from the Irish seas. Francis leaped into the thick of the fight, where the white-bearded captain was fighting with maniacal ferocity. He clove one man to the midriff, lopped off another's arm—and that laugh of his rang out shrill above the combat.

It was that laugh that struck terror into the hearts of their assailants. They fled to their galley, and Francis raced after them, cutting them down as they tried to scramble to safety. And then suddenly the Moorish galley was sailing before the wind, and the enemy had vanished.

The old captain came up to Francis and clapped him on the shoulder. He spoke in Arabic, which Francis didn't understand as he faced him, nude to the waist, filthy, and reeking with blood.

"My son!" said the old man, and took Francis in his arms.

"Nay, only a Frankish slave, my father!" Francis could see hate blaze out of the eyes of the slim young Moor who stood beside the old man.

"My son!" said the old captain again.

CHAPTER III

Guardian of an Old Man's Love

HE WAS none other than the deposed king of Granada, Muley Hassan. A veteran sea-fighter, he had himself transported Henry Tudor to England, to make his bid for the throne, believing that Tudor Richmond would support him, in return, against the power of Ferdinand and Isabella, the Spanish sovereigns, who were now menacing the Moorish kingdom with conquest.

Muley Hassan was in an extraordinary and undignified position. Once regnant King of Granada, it was his infatuation for the beautiful Spanish woman, known as Zorayah, the Morning Star, that had brought about his downfall. His wife, Aisha, had appealed for aid to the powerful clan of the Abencerrages, and Muley Hassan had been driven from his throne, which had been bestowed upon their son Boabdil, the weakling who now was king of Granada.

It was several years after landing on the Moorish coast before Francis saw Granada. In those years he made his name dreaded among the Spaniards in border fighting. Now he was being summoned home, because the Spanish sovereigns, Ferdinand and Isabella, were camped on the Vega, opposite Granada, and were erecting a besieging city, stone by stone.

Old Muley Hassan rode down on his white mule to greet Francis in person at the gate of the Albaicin quarter. Beside him rode his son, scowling Prince Yussef, the younger brother of King Boabdil.

Muley Hassan had come back to Granada with a certain Abdul Rachman, an Englishman, once known as Francis Blount, on whom he had bestowed his favors, to the rage of his son, black-bearded Yussef. He had advanced him to a high post in the Moorish army. And the Moors called this Englishman mad.

For none but a madman walked by himself and muttered. And none held his life so cheap, or had slain so many Spaniards in single combat. But it was principally that laugh of his that convinced the Moors that he was mad. He laughed at the learned doctors of the Law who sought to convert him to the Prophet's teachings. Wherefore this Abdul Rachman remained a Mozarebe, that is to say a Christian in the Moorish service, and therefore suspect.

Flags flew and trumpets sounded, All Granada had left its work to mass the streets and cheer as the procession wound up toward that incredible fortress of the Alhambra that Francis had never seen before. High above the Vega towered that stupendous fortress, with its walls and thirteen towers, rising to the Citadel, perched like an eyrie at the edge of the northwestern precipice.

Through shouting crowds they rode; then, dismounting, they left their horses at the Horse-Shoe Gate and proceeded afoot till they reached the great square before the fortress, where troops were drawn up amid frowning cannon. They passed into the palace-citadel, through the Court of the Mosques, the Court of the Myrtles, into the Hall of the Ambassadors, where a crowd was massed against the slender columns and delicately colored traceries.

Side by side upon two thrones were seated King Boabdil and his mother, Aisha. The thin-bearded Moorish sovereign rested motionless, his arms on the gilt arms of his throne. His mother was a veiled, fantastic figure, looking out upon the scene through the eye-slits of her veil.

"This, Caliph, is the young man Abdul Rachman, who has performed such deeds of valor," said Muley Hassan, presenting Francis.

Francis laughed. Because all this was unreal, and nothing was real except that spread of white roses under the trellis at Castle Eastover. He saw the shocked faces of the tribe of the Abencerrages, standing about the throne—and laughed again.

LATER, in a cool, tiled room of the General's Palace, Muley Hassan sat on a low divan, sipping sherbet, with Francis at his side.

"I have loved you as a son, Abdul Rachman, ever since that day when you fought beside me on the galley," said the old Moor. "I am an old man, and I have been King of Granada. My son Boabdil has ousted me from my throne, and my other son, Yussef, has never given me love. Now I want peace more than anything else.

"You, as the captain of my bodyguard, will protect me when I go abroad as Captain of the Alhambra. And your other task will be to see that none but myself enters the fortress of the Alcazaba."

He gestured toward the steep citadel at the end of the line of fortifications. And there was not a man but knew that in the Citadel lived Zorayah, the beautiful Spaniard, the Morning Star, for whose sake Muley Hassan had thrown away his throne.

Muley Hassan handed Francis a great key. And then, through the silence, Francis could hear the sound of hammers on stone, coming from across the Vega.

It was the sound of the masons of the Spanish sovereigns, Ferdinand and Isabella, building the besieging city of Santa Fé. Francis looked at Muley Hassan, and saw that he, too, knew that it portended the downfall of Granada.

HE, Francis Blount, was now the guardian of an infatuated old man's love. In which pursuit, he made his daily and nightly round of the towers, somewhere within which dwelled the beautiful Morning Star, Zorayah.

Pacing the road one evening, Francis became aware of two figures standing at the base of a mass of rocks that seemed to underlie the foundations of the Alcazaba. They were standing, a man and woman, where there seemed to be no possible standing place. As Francis drew back, he saw the figure of the woman vanish in the darkness, while the man seemed to move downward toward the sheer edge of the precipice.

Francis leaped across the rocks that separated him from the man, who, he could now see, wore the dress of a Spaniard. "Halt, sir!" he shouted, brandishing his scimitar.

The Spaniard turned with a snarl, clutching a sword that he had drawn from beneath his cloak. Twice their blades clashed and struck fire, and then Francis got home. The white edge of the scimitar caught the Spaniard across the neck and all but decapitated him. The corpse rolled down the rocks, bounded, rebounded, and dropped straight down to the Vega.

Then something flashed past Francis's face—a dagger, clattering on the rocks. He heard a cry from among them, leaped upward, and caught the woman who stood glaring at him. Her blonde loveliness told him that she could be nobody but Zorayah, the Morning Star.

She writhed in his grasp. The white shroud of a garment that she wore parted, revealing her lovely breasts. Francis felt the scent and sweetness of her as he held her.

"You killed him!"

"Your lover?"

Zorayah laughed bitterly. "I have no lover. But I would take one if he would give me my heart's desire."

"What is that?"

"Freedom, and death for the old fool, Muley Hassan!"

ONE of the chief reasons advanced by the Moors that Francis — Abdul Rachman — was mad, was that he had never had a mistress. He was unhuman, because women did not appeal to him at all. And many a pair of black eyes had looked wantonly and with provocation at the hero of the frontier skirmishes, whose deeds of valor had made him an almost legendary figure.

Always the face of Alayne had been before Francis. Always in his mind the thought that some day he would return to England to claim her. And always the knowledge that his life was cast in Granada, and that England was a forgotten dream.

Now, feeling Zorayah's soft arms about his neck, Francis remembered that he was a man.

And, laughing, he tore apart that white shroud of a garment and gazed upon her milk-white form, and bent his face toward the petals of her mouth, and heard the quickening of her breath. Then moon and stars faded, and the dim sounds from the Vega, far beneath, ceased to be audible, and Francis was only conscious of Zorayah's soft, pliant form in his arms, moulding itself against him until it became an engine of torment, drawing him down into an inferno of physical strife.

Much later the swimming night and stars came back into Francis's consciousness again. He flung the woman from him, and laughed. He strode up toward the Alcazaba, the Citadel.

CHAPTER IV

"Death to the Dogs!"

NOW it appeared that Their Catholic Majesties, Ferdinand and Isabella, who were besieging Granada, proposed to treat with it for its capitulation. They were sending an embassy, including one Ponce de Leon, and the English ambassador, who was none other than my lord Baron Eastover.

For Henry Tudor, now Henry VII of England, was planning a marriage between his eldest son, Arthur, and the daughter of the Spanish rulers, and he had no gratitude whatever toward old Muley Hassan, whose ships had

"I've come back for you as I promised!" he laughed. He caught her in his arms and carried her out, struggling.

enabled him to win the English throne.

Francis, captain of Muley Hassan's bodyguard, laughed as he stood in the Hall of the Ambassadors, in the Alhambra, and heard the proposal tossed back and forth among the chiefs of the Abencerrages, before those two incredible figures on the two thrones, King Boabdil and his mother, Aisha.

In the end, it was decided to receive the embassy at the Alhambra. Whereby it became Francis's duty to escort it from the city of Granada up to the Alhambra.

Francis rode down with his troop, to find the embassy assembled in the market-place, with Don Ponce de Leon, and old Baron Eastover, and his son, Philip. He bade them welcome, and ushered them up the hill toward the Alhambra.

Baron Eastover sat uncomfortably upon his horse. He didn't like these foreign lands, and he hadn't wanted the Spanish embassy, but had been persuaded to accept it. The young sprig, Philip, Alayne's brother, thrust his curled red shoes into his stirrups, adjusted his plumed cap, and smiled at the gaping throng. And, when he saw them, all the latent bitterness in Francis's heart became a flame of wrath.

These two had lurked securely in their homes when he rode out to fight for Richard Crookback, King of England. Francis remembered something he had said that evening when he tore down the white roses from the trellis at Castle Eastover:

"I shall come back for you, Alayne."

A vain boast, long since dismissed from memory, but the dark beauty of Lady Alayne was still in Francis's memory.

Baron Eastover and Philip didn't know him, of course. How could they have expected to see him there? How recognize the Francis Blount of old in this suntanned, war-hardened warrior in Moorish dress, at the head of his cavalry?

Francis, riding on the near side of Baron Eastover's horse, looked with amusement at the old statesman's face.

"That young Moor reminds me somewhat of Francis Blount," said young Sir Philip, as he rode at his father's side.

"Francis Blount? That young fool? Why, his bones have long since been mouldering in the Welsh Marches," replied the Baron.

"But there was the tale that he was trepanned aboard a Moorish galley," said Philip. "Goodman Carpenter and the fletcher-maker swore that they saw it. Now, what if this young man should be none other than Francis Blount, in service with the Moors?" he laughed.

My lord Eastover glanced at Francis's impassive face and smiled.

"He does not understand a word of what you are saying, Philip," he answered. "This young Moor has a certain resemblance to the young fool we knew, but your suggestion savors to me of fantasy."

SIR PHILIP thrust his curled red shoes further into his stirrups. The points curled up so far that he had little gold chains to fasten them about his calves. The age of the dandy was, in fact, just dawning.

"I was but jesting, father," answered Philip. "Francis Blount is long since with God, I trust, poor young man."

"I should advise you not to repeat this jest to your sister Alayne, when we return to Santa Fé," said Baron Eastover. "I have thought sometimes that Alayne hath never forgot that young fool, Francis Blount."

So they talked, while Francis rode impassively at their side, and listened, and knew that Alayne was in Santa Fé, the besieging city that the Spanish sovereigns were erecting across the Vega, opposite Granada.

And then he knew that his boast had not been in vain. Alayne should yet be his. The years rolled back. He laughed wildly, and spurred his horse forward, while Baron Eastover and his son looked after him in astonishment.

"But what is the matter with your captain?" the Baron asked the interpreter.

"Excellency, the young man is a most valiant soldier, but at times God afflicts him with a strange frenzy, and then he laughs in his madness."

"It seems strange," said Lord Eastover frigidly, "that your

Caliph should send a madman to escort us to his audience."

IN THE great square Hall of the Ambassadors, the embassy bent low before the figures of King Boabdil and his mother, Aisha. Eastover saw the dark, scowling faces of the Abencerrages about them, and was glad of the protection of the troop of guards under Francis.

Through the interpreter, Baron Eastover said: "His puissant Grace, my sovereign, Harry 7th, by the Grace of God, King of the realms of England, Wales, Ireland, and France, being distressed by the querrel between Your Mightiness and Their Most Catholic Majesties of the Spanish realms, hath empowered me to mediate. These be the terms proposed."

Baron Eastover handed a letter to King Boabdil, but his mother took it.

"And," continued the Englishman, "Their Most Catholic Majesties wish Your Mightiness to know that your fleet of galleys from Barbary has been destroyed in a sea-battle with the Genoese, and there is no further hope for Granada, save in surrender. My sovereign, as a merciful liege, remembers past favors from your House, and wishes to protect it in its extremity."

Bold words! Bold words to utter in the Alhambra, that had been the centre of Morrish rule for centuries. Cries of anger and disbelief broke from the Abencerrages. They clutched the hilts of their swords and muttered. On their two thrones, Aisha and Boabdil sat motionless, poring over the letter, the sparsely bearded face and the veiled head together.

"If Your Excellencies will retire for a brief space, you shall have our answer," said Aisha.

Francis conducted the envoys into the Court of the Myrtles, and left his escort with them. Then he strolled back.

He saw that in the brief interval of his absence some plan had been debated. One of the chiefs of the Abencerrages said directly:

"We kill these dogs of Christians and proclaim a Holy War through all the lands of the Crescent. How say you, Abdul Rachman?"

Old Muley Hassan, on the other side of the throne, said stoutly, "My hands shall not be stained with murder."

"And so say I," said Francis.

"Death to the dogs!" shouted the Abencerrages.

THAT laugh of Francis struck terror into them. They feared this man, whose deeds were legendary. They knew that his followers would stand by him.

Spade-bearded, Prince Yussef, Muley Hassan's second son, sprang forward, pointing a long finger at Francis.

"Do you still trust this man?" he cried. "Is he not a Mozarebe, an infidel, and one at heart with the infidels? Kill, I say! Kill!"

"And I say," answered Francis, "that to murder an ambassador would be to proclaim our degradation to the whole world. Raise no hand against these men, or my troop will stand by them to the last."

There followed silence then.

Aisha and Boabdil whispered together on their thrones. Aisha looked at Francis through the slits in her veil.

"The demand," she said in her thin voice, "is that Granada surrender to the infidels, under guarantee of life and property. How would you answer?"

"I should refuse," said Francis. "Then I should collect all the troops we can muster, and fall upon Santa Fé and destroy it, and restore the Moslem power in Spain."

Some of the Abencerrages still scowled, but others shouted. It might be that the advice of the madman was not so bad after all.

Aisha looked at her councillors. "If that be your agreement, my lords, we will dismiss the envoys with a courteous refusal," she said.

To the ambassadors, recalled, she said, "Tell their Majesties in Santa Fé that Granada rejects and scorns their demand for surrender. Tell them we shall meet war with war."

Baron Eastover, as an English gentleman, evinced no surprise. He bowed, as did the others. Francis rode with them out through the entrance to the Alhambra. He took his leave at the gate of the Albaicin quarter.

It was very silent in the Alhambra. The sentries trod their rounds, but the whole vast building, with its seven courts, might have been dead. The murder that had been averted yet seemed to brood ominously over the fortress-palace.

Francis knew that it needed only a whim, an impulse, for the strange, throned pair to destroy both Muley Hassan and himself. He had aroused an enmity that could be quelled only by blood.

CHAPTER V

The Slave-Market

THE General's Palace was dark, but from beyond the aloe hedge there was a light in the guard-house of the Alcazaba. The great cresset-lamp in front of it threw a pale, luminous aureole upon the ground. Far underneath stretched the plain of the Vega, like an empurpled sea. In the dis-

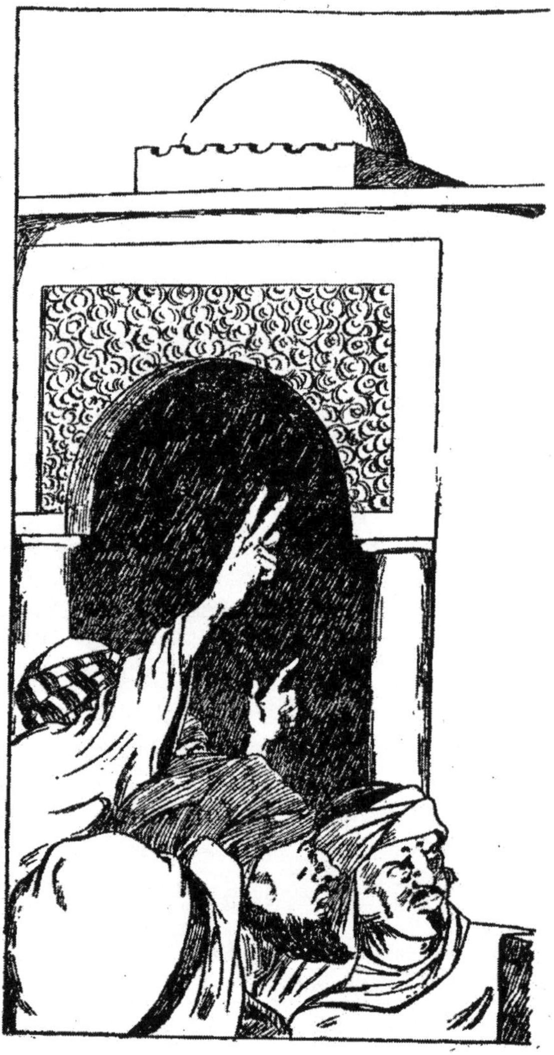

tance stood up the white peaks of Veleta and Mulhacen. Far below were the lights of Granada.

Francis, on guard, moved forward as he saw the woman's figure move out of the crevice in the rocks. Zorayah stood before him.

"Ah, the brave Captain of the Guard!" she mocked. "The Captain of the Guard of that old man who thinks I am his prisoner here."

"I remember you, madam."

"You remember my embraces?" laughed Zorayah. "But do you think I am unaware that the Abencerrages hate you? Aye, and Queen Aisha and her kinglet, too?"

"It is most men's misfortune to make enemies, madam."

"Mock me not. You are a Christian, and therefore suspect. And you are a fool. Each day that you tarry here your life is in danger. There is a secret entrance to this Citadel, up which the Romans once

"A thousand!" cried Francis, bidding for the girl he himself had put up for sale.

marched four abreast. I know it. Now, do we work together? Does the love of Zorayah, the Morning Star, mean anything to you?"

She flung her white robes from her, and stood before him in all the beauty of her womanhood. And then the memory of Alayne faded from Francis's mind.

He drew Zorayah into his arms. He felt the firm pressure of her breasts against him. And then, as before, there was neither moon nor stars, nor anything except the clinging pressure of Zorayah's body.

LATER she detached herself, and disappeared among the rocks at the base of the Citadel. Francis came back to sanity. He hated her now, this woman who had disrupted his memories of Alayne, for whose sake Muley Hassan had thrown away his dominions.

He strode to the guard-house of the Alcazaba, and hammered on the door. "There is work afoot," he shouted. "Who rides with me?"

He laughed, this madman, while the guard stood gaping at him. "There is death to face," he said, "unless we work swiftly and well. In brief, we go to Santa Fé to make a hostage of a lady who attends upon the queen of Castile. Who comes with me?"

"I come!"

"And I."

"And I!"

"We'll follow you to hell, Abdul Rachman!"

"Aye, we'll follow the Christian to hell, since hell must be his final portion!"

"For a lady too. Our Christian has changed his colors since the old days, when he foreswore ladies!"

Thus his men jested roughly, but Francis laughed.

"About the time of moonrise saddle your horses, but do not armor them," he said. "Wear only helm, corselet, and armpiece, for we must ride lightly. Each man his scimitar and two pistols. Be ready when I come for you."

Francis sat down on the edge of the precipice, staring across the Vega, which lay like blackest night beneath him. The lights of Granada were beginning to go out, but far away there shone a galaxy from the Spanish sovereigns' city of Santa Fé.

Francis sat there long, while the stars circled overhead. Then at last the edge of the moon appeared in the east; it rose, and the full orb swung low over the horizon. He heard the stamping of the horses in their stalls, and the cries of his men adjusting saddles and bridles, the clank of armpiece and corselet.

Francis ran into the guard-room and stood bare-headed and unarmored there.

"Form by twos. Straight down the Citadel and across the Vega. And follow me always!"

"Your helm! Your corselet, Captain!"

"Bah, this is no time for trifles!" Francis sneered.

LED by their madman, the troop rode along the battlements. The great gates of the Alhambra swung open at Francis's command. They passed through the Horse-Shoe Gate, then swung out across the Vega.

Francis halted them. "Here is the great cross in the center of Santa Fé," he said. "Here, facing it, is the palace of the King and Queen. We ride and fight like madmen, for I doubt whether we shall return."

They rode on over the dark Vega. Twice a sentry leaped out of the dark, his cross-bow presented, and each time the stroke of a scimitar struck him down. The lights of Santa Fé twinkled ahead, and the great cruciform city began to take shape in the darkness.

A sleepy picket that challenged at the outskirts of the town was ridden down before it could give the alarm. The charge of the Moorish troopers swept over the dozing sentries and cut down the guard before the palace, which now lay open to attack.

"Stand by your horses! Wait for me!" cried Francis, and ran from room to room, thrusting back the sleepy cavaliers who came tumbling out, half-dressed. Frantic women ran screaming along the corridors, and Francis, seizing each one by her shoulders, stared into her face, and flung her away with that legendary laugh of his, because she wasn't Alayne.

He bounded up the stairs, past screaming wenches and frantic serving-men. And then at last he found Alayne. She stood confronting him, in her nightrobe of white linen, open in the front, with her breasts heaving beneath it, milk-white despite the dark.

And, at the sight of her, Francis felt a thrill of exultation. Baron Eastover's daughter, and only a woman after all! Better if she had yielded herself to him long ago in England! He didn't want her now. Memories of Zorayah still stirred in him. He looked at her with hatred.

"I have come back for you as I promised," Francis gibed. "Dress yourself on the instant, madam!"

"You are still the same fool as ever, Francis Blount," said Alayne, recognizing him.

Francis saw, almost at his feet, a furred robe that some woman had flung down in the scramble for safety. He flung it about Alayne's shoulders, and caught her in his arms, while she screamed and beat at his face. He carried her, struggling, down the stairway.

"Mount and away!" he roared, and swung Alayne into the saddle before him.

Then he saw something that aroused him to seething anger. On Alayne's finger was the great diamond ring that he had lost on Bosworth Field.

"I bought it for a trifle, hoping some day to restore it to you," cried Alayne.

Francis tore off the stone and put it on his own finger. His mother's legacy, his only patrimony.

The Spaniards were gathering in Santa Fé, and muskets began to crack, but already Francis's troop was racing across the Vega.

ALAYNE had ceased to struggle. A score of Spanish cavaliers, who had hastily assembled, went down like paper before the Moorish charge. Santa Fé lay behind. Now dawn was coming up over the Vega. The great white peaks of Mulhacen and Veleta stood out rosy against the line of the Sierras. The massive structure of the Alhambra frowned darkly upon the hill, and beyond Granada, sprawling across the level plain, the sky was turning saffron.

Moorish sentries sprang up and challenged, soldiers gathered about the troop, cheering, and peering at the woman who lay in Francis's arms.

For the tale of the night raid was already common knowledge. For the sake of a woman, the woman-hating Abdul Rachman had led his troop into Santa Fé itself. It was another of those exploits that surrounded the name of the Mozarebe with glamor.

It was light now. The sun hung, a great ball, in the east. And all Granada was astir, for the early hours were the hours of business. The call to the dawn prayers was being chanted from the minarets of the mosques. Craftsmen were in their shops, the slave and cattle-markets were filling, carts were bringing in vegetables, oranges and pomegranates.

Down from the Alhambra men were swarming to greet this new exploit of Abdul Rachman. Crowds gathered about the little troop as it pushed its way forward through the outlying districts of the town.

Where was Abdul Rachman taking this woman whom he had snatched from the camp of the infidels? She lay so inertly in his arms, and on the face of Abdul Rachman was a look that made all shudder.

As Francis rode, straight into the heart of the town, toward the great slave and cattle-markets, the hoof-clacks of his men behind him, there sprang into remembrance terrible old stories of the days before the Law. Stories of human sacrifice to the old gods. Was it the

purpose of this Mozarebe to sacrifice this woman at the altar of a mosque, as one sacrificed sheep to Allah?

That look upon Abdul Rachman's face was terrible in its intensity.

CHAPTER VI

A Test of Strength

THERE was still trade in the slave-market, for pirate galleys still slipped past the Spanish blockading fleet and landed their human wares. The

Sword bared, Francis cried: "Again I say this woman is mine, and I claim her!"

morning auction was just opening, and a crowd had assembled to watch the proceedings. The auctioneer, an enormously fat Moor, with his two Nubian assistants, was intoning the prayer after the thin-bearded little *imam:*

"We praise and bless Thee, Allah, the Merciful, the Compassionate, for all Thy creatures here assembled.

"We praise and bless Thee, asking for a good market, just weight and measure for all merchandise, and strength of limb and sinew for all slaves subject to Thy law, and grace and comeliness for all women-slaves."

The seats opposite the raised platform were beginning to fill with grave-visaged Moorish merchants.

Two Jewish money-changers were setting up their booths nearby. The auctioneer strode across the platform to one of the two wooden structures that housed the male and female slaves, and hauled out a squealing negress.

He pulled her into the center of the dais. Gold bangles jangled on her wrists, and her white garment fluttered in the morning breeze, revealing the sinuous curves of her ample form.

"Here is a slave-girl worthy of a pasha's home," he shouted. "No more than twenty years of age, docile and well trained to housework. Step up and see her teeth; they are sound and white as a hound's. Feel the muscles of her arm; they are as strong as a man's. Who bids?"

"Fifty moidores," said one of the merchants.

"Fifty? For this wench who will serve you and your sons, and their sons' sons for fifty years to come? Who bids?"

"Seventy," said another.

"Seventy-five," said the first, and there were no other bidders.

Hardly had the negress been disposed of when the shouting of the mob that followed Francis broke out. Over the mud walls of the *sokh* the crowd could be seen streaming.

Francis appeared, riding a sweat-stained horse, with a woman, covered with a furred robe, held in his arms.

Still holding her, he leaped out of his saddle, ascended the three steps to the dais, and set her on her feet.

"Here is a slave whom I have captured from the infidel city of Santa Fé," he shouted. "Let her be sold, auctioneer, in accordance with the provisions of the Moslem law!"

UNTIL that moment Alayne had not understood what Francis planned to do. Now she stood tottering, staring in utter unbelief into his face. In it she saw only madness and hatred. By now Francis's troopers were in the *sokh*, sitting their horses about the dais. And the market itself was packed with a jesting, jostling throng, whose movements filled the air with dust from the trampled floor.

A roar went up, one universal roar of admiration. This capped all Abdul Rachman's exploits, that he should have taken one of Queen Isabella's waiting-women from the palace itself, and should have brought her to Granada, to be sold for a slave. There was no pity in a single one of those faces turned upon Alayne. Only staring eyes, and mouths agape with laughter.

Francis wrenched at the girl's furred robe and rent her night attire, exposing her white bosom to the brutal throng. Then, as she struck at him, he hit her in the face.

"Sell this slave!" he roared to the auctioneer. "I have looked for this day for many years, since this woman let me go to my death, a foolish boy, in England! Hold her, you men!"

The two Nubians, giant men, nude to the waist, came forward, beads of sweat glistening on their brown bodies.

Alayne stood up, proudly indifferent to the grinning crowd, drawing her furred robe about her. The wealthier merchants licked their lips as they looked at her. A white-skinned woman with dark hair, and of the most beauteous form. A prize for a rich, doddering old pasha.

A little crowd of soldiers was pushing through the mob. Behind them, Francis saw Prince Yussef and two of the chiefs of the Abencerrages. Prince Yussef seated himself opposite the dais.

"Well, auctioneer," cried Francis again, "here is a slave who should bring you a rich commission. Look upon her, gentlemen—have you ever seen her peer?"

"But he is taking my job away from me," grumbled the auctioneer.

HE TURNED to Alayne. "Well, it seems that good fortune has come to someone here today," he cried. "Look at her. A white-skinned woman from the north. Dare I open her mouth to show her teeth? No, she would bite me! Proud, high-strung, fiery, like a Barbary horse! Who bids? Who bids?"

"Three hundred moidores!" cried a merchant.

"Four hundred!"

"Five."

"I bid a thousand," said Francis, impelled by some motive he could himself not understand.

"What? He bids for her himself? It was for himself, then, that Abdul Rachman stole the wench from Santa Fé palace!" They muttered and grumbled. Then one of the merchants cried:

"Your pardon, Abdul Rachman, but the law of the *sokh* is that all money must be shown, unless there is property on which a bond may be given."

Francis walked to one of the Jews at the money-booths. "How much for this?" he asked, displaying the great stone on his finger.

"Fifteen hundred moidores," said the Jew breathlessly.

"Two thousand," shouted the second Jew, who had come running up to see.

"I bid twelve hundred moidores for the girl," cried Prince Yussef, standing up.

"Fifteen hundred," said Francis.

"Sixteen hundred."

"Two thousand!"

The two men looked at each other, and all the old hate flamed out between them.

"I am offered two thousand moidores—I am offered two thousand moidores," chanted the auctioneer.

"You are offered twelve hundred moidores," said spade-bearded Yussef, gathering his cloak about him. "This other bid is void."

"But why—but why, my lord?" queried the auctioneer.

"Because this other bidder, Abdul Rachman, is a Mozarebe, a Christian serving under Moorish rule, and it is the law of the Prophet that no infidel can hold a slave, not even an infidel slave."

THE slave-market was full of armed men now, members of the clan of the Abencerrages, outnumbering Francis's troop by five to one. Francis looked about him, and saw the trap.

"I appeal to the Caliph!" he shouted. And moved between his men and the Abencerrages, who were drawing their scimitars.

Prince Yussef bowed ironically. "You shall go to the Caliph," he answered. "He is the exponent of Islam."

"Aye, but I take this slave-woman with me."

"She shall be brought before the Caliph," Yussef mocked. One of his men raised Alayne upon a horse before him. She seemed to have fainted, and the furred robe, gaping wide, revealed her white form, almost bare to the waist. Jeers, mockery, and desire—the dusty *sokh*—the Abencerrages, galloping in the wake of Prince Yussef—and Francis gnashing his teeth as he realized that he had overreached himself.

One of his troopers touched him on the arm. "We fight for you to the end, Abdul Rachman," he said. Yet I would counsel you to yield this slave-woman to Prince Yussef."

"How so?"

"Because King Boabdil and his mother have failed our country. They have remained idle since the Spaniards began to build their city upon the Vega. Patience—a little patience, and we shall restore Muley Hassan to his throne, and then regain our kingdom."

Then Francis laughed again, sitting his horse in the midst of his troop.

"If you will follow me," he said, "and fight for me, we shall see the judgment of this matter."

His troop of eleven men rode behind him, up through the streets of Granada, up to the Horse-Shoe Gate, and so along the ramparts to the Alhambra.

Old Mulet Hassan met them alone, wearing his armor, with his white beard flowing down over his breast.

"This is a great deed you have done, my son," he said, embracing Francis. "But tell me now, what is this story of the slave-woman in the *sokh*, and how did it happen that you let my traitor son, Yussef, win her away from you?"

CHAPTER VII

The Secret Exit

IN THE cool of the afternoon, in the Hall of the Ambassadors, King Boabdil, with his mother enthroned beside him, was delivering judgment to the petitioners grouped before him.

Alayne was standing back against the delicate tracery of the wall, in her furred robe. About her were grouped the chiefs of the Abencerrages. Yussef was eyeing her speculatively. It had been his hatred of Francis that had inspired his action in the *sokh*, but now he was thinking that he had invested his moidores very prudently.

"Caliph, this woman is mine," said Francis to the King. "Last night I took her from the palace at Santa Fé. I claim her, therefore, by right of capture, and none shall take her from me."

Prince Yussef strode forward. "This woman is mine by right of purchase in the open market," he said. "For this Abdul Rachman is a Christian Mozarebe, and therefore not permitted to own a slave."

Muttering laughter came from the Abencerrages. The little band of Francis's troopers laid their hands upon their scimitars. The old quarrel was ready for settlement now, when Granada was about to fall apart like a ripe pome-

Suddenly Zorayah rushed at him with a screech, a raised dagger in her hand. . . .

granate. Francis glanced at old Muley Hassan, and saw his eyes flash fire. Then at those two figures on their thrones, whispering together, while the Abencerrages waited, and Alayne stood in their midst, a white pillar of beauty. Then Boabdil leaned forward.

"We adjudge this slave-woman to you, brother," he addressed Yusef, "since Moslem law does not permit a Mozarebe to hold a slave."

THERE was an interlude of tense and utter silence, while the two parties watched each other and waited. The first move was Francis's. He leaped it to Alayne's side as she stood swaying against the tracery of the wall. Most of what had happened to her in that incredible night was incomprehensible, but she realized now that this was Francis Blount again, with the madness gone from his eyes.

"Again I say this woman is mine, and I claim her!" Francis shouted. "For, having captured her to be a slave, I release her from slavery. If I have ever served you, Mightiness, remember that!"

Out of the ensuing silence the tumult broke, swiftly, violently, and yet as if time had in some manner been slowed down, so that for an instant there was only a tiny stir, and hands seemed to go to the hilts of scimitars negligently, indolently. Just for an instant that illusion lasted. Then, with an outburst of fierce cries, Prince Yussef's men sprang forward, and Francis's eleven troopers and Muley Hassan closed in about him.

The Abencerrages outnumbered Francis's men by three and four to one, but even the boldest of them hesitated in the face of their former King, standing beside that legendary figure that laughed as it slew. And Francis's laugh rang out as Prince Yussef, thrust forward despite himself, dropped with cloven shoulder and riven torso, so that he fell, instantly dead, in a heap of bloody rags that had been the apparel of a prince.

The body dropped at Francis's feet, and Francis thrust back Alayne behind him, and raised his scimitar to meet the savage onslaught. For an instant the tribesmen hesitated, and then flung themselves on Francis's eleven troopers. Three and four to one—but Francis's men wore helm, corselet, and shoulder-piece, off which the strokes of the hostile scimitars glanced. Blades were thrust into black-bearded faces, and Francis's laugh rang out more than once as he toppled an Abencerrage to death.

Now the little band was beating back its enemies. It cut a bloody swath through them, and those of the palace guards as they came rushing into the battle. And ever at its head fought Francis and the doughty old warrior, Muley Hassan, standing beside him, leaping forward, and delivering great slicing thrusts with his great sword.

THEY had driven the Abencerrages to flight into the Court of the Lions adjacent, with its colored tiles of blue and gold, and the twelve marble lions supporting the great alabaster basin with its fountain. More than one massacre had stained the Alhambra's floors with blood in bygone days. But there had never been a fight so grotesque as this.

For those two unbelievable figures were still upon their thrones. Sparse-bearded King Boabdil was leaning forward eagerly, watching, but Aisha seemed hardly to have stirred, though she had just seen Yussef, her younger son, struck down at her feet. Not a cry came from her lips; only her black eyes peered eagerly through the slits of her head-dress.

Then suddenly Muley Hassan, his armor splashed with the blood of dead men, paused, and moved a few feet back to where Prince Yussef lay, and a great cry broke from his lips.

"My son, my son!" he moaned, and caught the body in his arms. For a moment he stood thus, looking at Aisha on her throne upon the dais. Husband and wife, once King and Queen, and their dead son between them—and the other seated by the woman, fingering his sparse beard.

For a moment they watched each other—they two who were never to meet again. This was the summation of their lives, this was the ripened fruit of folly, which old Muley Hassan cast from him as suddenly as he had clasped it to his breast.

There was something magnificent in the last days of Granada. There was something bigger than love or life. It was the soul of a nation, dying because there was none worthy to maintain it, but dying with a certain magnificence.

The troopers looked at their madman, the eight who still survived, though several of them were bleeding from sabre-gashes.

"And what now?" asked the sub-captain.

"Back to the Alcazaba! Hold it! Rally the troops for Muley Hassan, the lawful king of Granada!" Francis shouted.

HE WAS thrusting Alayne before him as he spoke, and she moved like a figure in a dream. She knew only that this was Francis Blount again, whom she had always loved. She was no longer conscious of fear, despite the shouting, blood-spattered figures about her, and the Abencerrages and guards lurking in the Court of the Lions adjacent.

Suddenly they smiled at each other, and knew that this play of life meant nothing. All that had ever meant anything had been the spray of white roses that Alayne had given Francis when he rode away to the wars, and perhaps that spray of white roses that he had torn down from the trellis in the close of Castle Eastover.

They smiled at each other, and Francis thrust Alayne before him. "Back to the Alcazaba!" he shouted. And then, to the mob of stupefied soldiers, "Here is your lawful King, Muley Hassan, of Granada!"

He thought afterward how easily he could have torn those two helpless puppets from their thrones, as they sat there, goggle-eyed at the slaughter.

Inside, the palace guards and the Abencerrages were reassembling; outside, the crowd shrank back before that blood-dripping scimitar of Francis's.

"Here is your King, Muley Hassan!" Francis shouted again.

There came no response. Silent and stunned, the soldiers watched him. But the stir within the palace was increasing. A cross-bow quarrel whizzed past Francis's head and clanged against the parapet of the ramparts.

"To the Alcazaba!" shouted Francis's sub-captain.

The ten men pushed their way along the ramparts toward it, through a throng that fell back before them, but watched them in the same stupefaction. Then out of the Alhambra there came a rush of palace guards, a shower of quarrels whirred, and scimitars were bared. That rush broke before the charge of the ten, and again they made their way along the ramparts, to the same silent, stupefied watch of the gathering soldiers.

(Continued on page 114)

Diana Daw
DIANA, SUFFERING FROM AMNESIA, BELIEVES HERSELF TO BE A CZECH SPY —
By CLAYTON MAXWELL

A FINE MESS TO BE IN -- HERE I AM IN A NAZI CONCENTRATION CAMP. FEW EVER COME OUT ALIVE, I HEAR!

I WONDER WHO THAT IS TALKING --- THEY MENTION "ESCAPE". I'LL JOIN THEM. THE TALKING IS COMING FROM BEHIND THAT SHACK!
--- AND WE CAN ESCAPE--

WHO ARE YOU?
A NAZI SPY -- THE CAMP'S FULL OF THEM, POSING AS PRISONERS!
KILL HER -- SHE OVERHEARD US!
PLEASE -- I'M NOT A NAZI!

KILL HER -- THE VILE SPY!
OUR CAREFULLY LAID PLANS WON'T GO WRONG THIS LATE!
PLEASE!
WAIT! PERHAPS SHE'S ONE OF US!

I'M A CZECH -- VILMA SMOLESKA -- I'M CONVICTED OF BEING A CZECH SPY -- I'M REALLY NOT A NAZI INFORMER!

WE'RE CZECHS, TOO. WE'LL HAVE TO TRUST YOU NOW -- YOU ALREADY KNOW TOO MUCH!
YOU CAN TRUST ME!
YEAH -- WE CAN'T KILL HER. THERE WOULD BE AN INQUIRY -- AND SO OUR PLAN WOULD PROBABLY COME OUT!

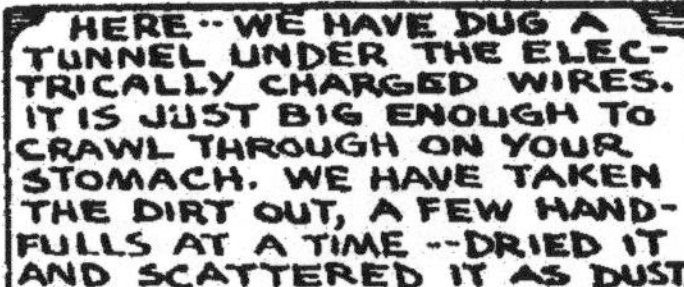

INSIDE A CRUDE HUT THE PLAN IS EXPLAINED TO HER

IT IS VERY SIMPLE, BUT ONE OF US MUST BE SACRIFICED SO THAT THE OTHERS MAY ESCAPE. ONE CREATES A DIVERSION ON ONE SIDE OF THE CAMP--THE SEARCHLIGHTS ARE TURNED THAT WAY---THE GUARDS RUSH THERE---AND WE ESCAPE OUT THE OTHER SIDE, THROUGH THE TUNNEL, DURING THE EXCITEMENT. I HAVE FOUR STRAWS HERE--WE DRAW--THE ONE WHO DRAWS THE SHORT ONE--CREATES THE DIVERSION AND RECEIVES FROM THE NAZI'S--DEATH, OF COURSE!

WHAT HAPPENS TO DIANA? SEE THE DECEMBER ISSUE OF SPICY ADVENTURE STORIES

SWAMP PRINCESS

PETE GARNER was staring ahead into the blackness of Cajun Swamp, holding onto his overturned pirogue and wondering what the hell could happen to him next, when the prow of the boat dug into the mudbank of a dark little island. Thankfully, he scrambled up onto dry ground, for it had been hard enough holding onto the slippery, slimy hull, wondering when one of the splashing alligators around him would take a snap at his legs, or what he was going to do now that the capsized boat had lost him his food supply and gun. There were water moccasins too, and he had thought about those as he shivered with the cold and tried to see what was ahead by the rays of a thin crescent moon which only emphasized the darkness of the bog.

Even now, his feet once more on dry ground, he cursed himself for having started on this venture. He was cold and uncomfortable, with wet clothes clinging to him and water squishing in his boots, and he was anxious to find out where he was. He stared through the near blackness, making out the ghostly shape of trees in the dim moonlight which hardly penetrated the foliage. Listening for a minute to the ceaseless croaking of frogs, he started forward, his face brushing against low-hanging Spanish moss.

Suddenly he saw a light, a pale flicker of yellow, and he quickened his pace. The trees shut out the light, and then after a moment he saw it again. And in the same instant, though he saw no one, he heard a quick step from the shadows, felt a gun muzzle. Close to his ear a whispered command:

"Put your hands up!"

Garner hesitated, then raised his arms and turned slowly. The faintest trickle of moonlight enabled him to make out a slim, dirty-faced youth in pulled down cap, tattered shirt and ragged overalls. And Garner could see only too clearly the hand gripping the butt of the automatic.

But where Pete expected to see grim eyes, there were large, soft blue ones, showing hesitancy, perhaps fear. This kid, Pete decided, was no killer—he wouldn't have the guts to pull the trigger. Ten years as a police reporter on New Orleans papers had given Pete plenty experience reading character from men's faces, and now he risked his life on his knowledge. He swept his right arm downward across the youth's gun wrist.

There was a sharp cry of pain and the gun fell to the ground. Pete grunted in triumph and grabbed at the frail figure of his assailant. The youngster pivoted desperately, tried to squirm away, but was caught in the hard circle of Pete's arm.

Pete felt the lad's tattered shirt

The woman of the swamp was beautiful, but she was a kidnaper, a jailbird. She was evil and she was dangerous. Pete Garner found that out . . .

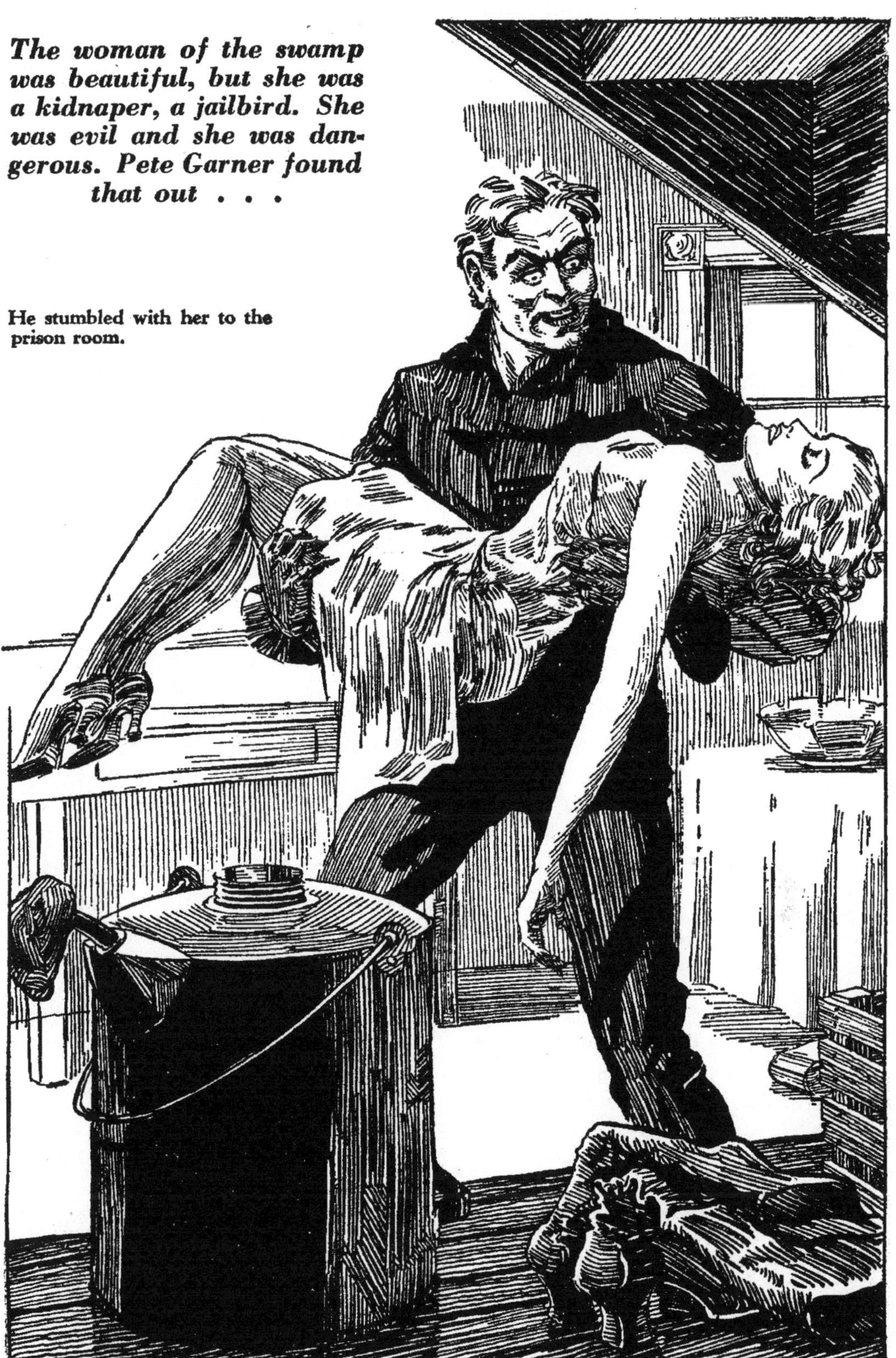

He stumbled with her to the prison room.

By ELLERY WATSON CALDER

come away in his grasping hand. He tightened his arms about his victim's heaving chest and lifted—Then suddenly he muttered, "I'll be damned!" and released his hold. That squirming figure wasn't a boy. . . . It was a slender young girl! In the struggle, Pete had torn not only her shirt, but a tight bandeau which had held her breasts tight against her body. Now in the faint moon rays he stared at the pale curved flesh which the dismayed girl tried to cover with her trembling hands.

SUDDENLY Pete stooped and found the dropped automatic. He said, "Maybe now you'll explain your idea in poking this in my ribs." His voice was grim, and he saw that the girl's face had gone white, her eyes wide and frightened.

Her dark hair was awry, loosened from where she had tucked it up under the concealing cap, and despite the grime-smudged features, he could see that she was pretty.

"I—I—" she stammered. Her red lips quivered, and Pete found it hard to make his voice stern. But after all, she'd poked a gun at him.

"Talk," he growled, "and talk fast."

The girl seemed to brace up. Bitterly, she demanded, "What can I say? I can't say anything to a dirty kidnaper. You know well enough what I wanted with the gun. Well, now you've got me—go ahead and lock me up in your shack, where you've got my father."

Pete started. He whispered, "What the devil do you mean?" But before she could answer, he had recognized her, from newspaper pictures he had seen. "Say—you're Sally Somers! The daughter of John Somers, the New Orleans banker who was kidnaped last month!"

"You ought to know all about it!" the girl flared sarcastically. Pete grinned.

"Baby, listen to me. I'm no member of the gang that's got your dad. I'm a reporter for the New Orleans *Picayune-Herald.* My name's Pete Garner."

"A—a reporter?"

"Sure. And the reason I'm here is that I got a hot tip from a stoolie that your father was being held somewhere near this swamp and I set out to try to find him myself and get a scoop. "But what," Pete asked, "are you doing here?"

With a gasp, Sally Somers glanced toward the point of light which had been Pete's destination. She said in a low voice, "I learned, too, that they had my father here, and I was trying to rescue him."

"You came into this swamp all by yourself?" Pete asked incredulously. But his eyes weren't on her face. He could not help noticing that she had forgotten to hold the tattered shirt together, and the small, rounded globes of her perfect breasts were almost entirely uncovered, trembling with her excited breathing.

"Of course," the girl said defiantly. "I had a gun, didn't I?"

Pete hefted the automatic. He smiled grimly. "Well, I've got it now, and I think I'll keep it. This is no toy for a kid like you."

She stepped close to him, her

eyes blazing. "I'm no kid—I'm twenty!"

Pete felt his heart hammering. Despite the man's costume, Sally had not erased a faint feminine fragrance which now reached his nostrils and reminded him that she was very young and very lovely. The torn overalls, too, now that he looked closely, revealed the rounded contours of slim hips, the outlines of long shapely legs. Pete felt an impulse to grab her, to crush her against him, to flatten the softly curved breasts against his thudding heart. . . . But he caught himself, remembering their surroundings, the danger, the work they had to do. With a grin, he reached out and pulled the torn shirt together.

"I could think up a plan better if there weren't so much to distract me," he said.

She might have been blushing, but it was too dark to see. She faltered, "What are you going to do?"

"Do? Why I'm going to rescue your father, of course. Do you know anything that might help me?"

SALLY nodded, pointing toward the light which Pete had for the moment forgotten. "I think they've got him in that cabin. I sneaked up and looked through the window a little while ago. I heard them talking—about a man they were expecting."

"You mean tonight?"

"Yes, they were waiting for someone—a member of the gang from New Orleans, who's supposed to tell them whether the ransom has been paid by my father's bank. Then they'll know whether to release him. Apparently—from what I could hear, they don't know him by sight, but I heard his name: Snapper Riley."

"And you must have thought I was this Riley, when you stuck the gun in my kidneys."

She nodded, and suddenly Pete snapped his fingers and said, "You were right! That's just who I am—as far as the gang in that cabin knows. If they don't know him by sight, I'll go in, palm myself off as Snapper Riley, tell them the ransom has been paid, and I'll take your father back to New Orleans!"

"Oh . . . Do you think you can do it? It'll be dangerous. I—I'm afraid for you. . . ."

Pete touched her hand, again resisted the impulse to draw her close. "Don't worry about me," he whispered tenderly. "I'll do it all right. Just you wait here while I go ahead."

Suddenly from behind him came a harsh, purring voice in Cajun-French accent. "*Mais non, mon ami!* You and zis gal will both go to zat cabin—you are my prisoners!"

Pete whirled, and from the shadows there stepped a hulking swampman cradling a sawed-off shotgun in the crook of his arm. As he stared into the leering, bearded features, the reporter felt his heart sink. Captured before he started! For this harsh-voiced brute with the shotgun must be a member of the gang of kidnapers.

"Drop the gun, *m'sieu!*" the fellow barked. "Before I, Pierre Valois, cut you in two with a charge of buckshot!"

But Pierre Valois's eyes were

licking over Sally's body, ferreting out the loveliness exposed by her torn shirt and overalls. Garner could guess what would happen to her when the Cajun got his hands on her, and he didn't like to think about it.

Nevertheless, he could only relax his fingers and let his gun slip to the ground. But at the same time he rapped out: "Sally — quick, shoot him with that other gun!"

It worked. The Cajun swung his shotgun automatically toward the girl, and as he turned, Pete plunged in, caught the swampman momentarily offguard with a smashing attack.

Before Valois could shift the shotgun, Pete had bashed him across the jaw. Holding the barrel of the gun aside with one hand, he thudded home another stiff jolt to the man's chin. Then he followed up his staggering prey—and followed too fast. The Cajun brought up his knee abruptly, and Pete twisted barely in time. Even so he felt momentarily faint from the blow, and he staggered back, remaining doubled over as if in agony, even as he recovered. Thinking his victim disabled, the Cajun rushed in, wide open, and Pete brought one up from the ground and hung it on the point of his jaw. The man sank like a log. Out.

AS PETE stepped back, Sally's arms were around him, and he could feel her trembling in fear. "Are you hurt?" she demanded. "You're all right?"

"Okay," he panted. But he didn't push her away. Her warm breasts were moulded to his chest, and behind their resilient cushion he could feel the rapid pulsing of her heart. In the wide eyes turned up to his was something that hadn't been there before — something for him, for a man who meant something to Sally Somers. Suddenly Pete let his arms close about the slender waist and he held her tight. The slim shapeliness of her legs through the overalls moved against him as she lifted herself to his kiss. Her mouth was moist and yielding to the caress of his own, and for a long, long moment she strained herself to him. Then she writhed out of his embrace, gasping, her bosom rising and falling spasmodically. Her eyes dropped.

Pete picked up the fallen shotgun and handed it to her. "Here." He heard his own voice harsh with emotion. "Stay here and guard this rat, while I go after your father. I'll bring him back if it's humanly possibly."

Sally met his eyes again. "I'll pray for you," she said fervently, softly.

Pete turned and moved rapidly toward the lighted window of the cabin. The water had leaked out of his boots by now and his feet made little noise on the ground. Approaching the ramshackle cabin he moved more cautiously and presently gained the window.

Slowly raising his eyes until he could see in, he discovered a barren, dirty looking front room, in the center of which was a crude table holding a lamp. At the table sat a man and a woman. The man was smooth-shaven, swarthy, evil faced. The woman— Pete gasped and his eyes dwelled in fascinated admiration on this woman he recognized from pictures he had seen in the rogue's gallery. She was Madelon LeClaire, mysterious swampland beauty who had been called Queen of the Cajuns and who was rumored to be the brains of the lawless element in this district. She had served time in the Federal jail at New Orleans for narcotic violations; she had been a thorn in the side of the police for years. But—Lord, she was beautiful!

Staring at her, Pete realized that the pictures hadn't done her justice. She had a long, lithe body, with the graceful feline movements of a cat. . . . Even her eyes, as she turned her head half toward him, were blazing pools, dark and deep, which somehow added to the catlike quality of her face. The passionate fullness of her lips, nearly blood red, the midnight blue-black of her hair, in such contrast to ivory-white skin . . . here was a woman, Pete realized, for whom men might easily murder!"

Seated at the table, she seemed to be clad in nothing but a thin silken robe, and Pete could see the generously rounded taut contours of her breasts, the mature sweep of her hips and, where the hem of the robe parted, the tapered length of one leg, smooth and creamy and long.

She was talking to her dark-faced companion, in a fluid, melodious Cajun-French voice. "Pierre has gone to meet this Snapper Riley," she said, "to guide him here. I think, however, that when Riley arrives, I shall insist on a change in our plans."

OUTSIDE the window, Pete Garner reflected that he would have to work fast if Riley had been expected so soon!

Madelon LeClaire continued. "A change in plans, *oui!* Even if Snapper Riley does bring the money, do we know it will be safe to release Somers and have him perhaps set the police on our trail? No—better it were, for this Riley to slit his gullet and dump him in the swamp for the 'gators."

Pete watched her and listened to the hardness come into her voice and he realized that, beautiful as she was, she was evil, this magnetic passionate woman was dark, soullessly evil. . . .

Well, if she could change her plans, he must change his own. He moved away from the window, fumbled until he found a broken tree-limb, and hurled it. It fell with a crash as he hastened to crouch beside the front door of the shack, and instantly the door opened. He heard the woman's command: "See what that noise is, Etienne." And her companion stepped out into the night, peering about.

Pete stepped forward noiselessly and clubbed the automatic down on the man's head. As the fellow dropped, Pete dragged him around behind the shack and then returned to the doorway. With automatic ready he stepped in.

At first he didn't see Madelon. Then he felt the muzzle of a gun punching his back, and her voice, clipped and hard, commanded: "I will take the gun, *m'sieu.*" She reached around and wrenched it from his hand. "Now turn around." He obeyed and shivered despite himself at the grim set of the mouth that could be passionate but could also be cruel. Her own gun was pointed at his heart as she demanded, "Tell me now—who are you?"

Pete shrugged. "I would have told you in another minute. My name's Snapper Riley. From New Orleans. I hope you don't greet all your guests with the artillery display."

"When they walk in with drawn guns, yes," the woman said. Her eyes were narrowed and suspicious. "Where is Valois, whom I sent to meet you? And where is Etienne, who just left?"

Pete Garner had talked himself out of tight spots before. He was in one now. He said easily, "They went back to bail out my pirogue. I upset it and spilled myself in the swamp. My clothes are all wet, as you see."

The Cajun woman's gun lowered a trifle. "You're Riley, eh? Very well, what message do you bring?"

"The ransom has been paid, and I've brought your share. I'm ready to take Somers back. Where is he?"

Madelon's red lips smiled, and it was a sinister smile. "You will do nothing of the kind, my friend. You will cut his throat and throw him to the 'gators. Thus we will have no police on our trail set by Mr. Somers. Now—give me the money."

Pete thought fast, and while he thought he let his eyes follow the invitation of the parted robe, which so temptingly displayed the pale, silk smooth skin of the Cajun Queen, the lush, swollen mounds of her breasts . . . the mature, lovely sweep of her hips and legs. . . . He smiled.

"Are you, then," he said half contemptuously, "that anxious to get the dough and split it with those other two?"

His eyes roved in hungry admiration over her body, and she saw this. Her voice was soft as she asked, "What do you mean by that, *m'sieu?*" Her own eyes measured the brawny masculine figure of the man in front of her.

"I'll tell you." Garner moved gently toward her. "You're beautiful . . . and you and I could live plenty high in some South American country—if we had the other two shares of the ransom to split between us. Why not?"

He closed the distance between them, hoping he could get his arms around her.

He had no trouble doing that. She said purringly, "I like bold men, Snapper Riley, especially bold rogues!"

She lowered the pistol a little more and somehow the thin robe fell further open. Her breasts trembled, her hips swayed in a slow, undulant challenge as he reached her and folded her in his arms. The pistol was completely lowered now, and her red lips parted and fastened with moist succulent caress to Pete's mouth. The straining, warm curvature of her body moved against him. . . .

Her mouth came away presently and she moaned. "Ah, *mon cher. . . !*" Her breath was warm against his cheek, against his throat as the wet trail of her lips sent flame leaping responsively through his veins.

But he made himself fight the

passion she was instilling in his unwilling blood. Stealthily his hand was reaching for the pistol in her hand.

And abruptly from the door a harsh Cajun voice rasped, "Madelon, you fool . . . *look out!*"

AS the woman flung herself from his embrace with a gasp, Pete whirled, cursing.

"Pierre!" Madelon cried. "What—what is it?"

Pete stared in dismay, for the bearded swampman in the doorway was the Cajun he had knocked out and left in Sally Somers' guard! And now the fellow was here; in his left hand was clenched strands of Sally's hair, and she had stumbled to her knees, half conscious, beside him.

"*Oui!*" The Cajun grinned. "You ask what is it, when you make love with an imposter—a newspaper reporter who came here to rescue John Somers. He is in league with this girl, here, who is Somers' daughter."

Despair and rage flooded Pete Garner. It was all up, now, just when he was about to succeed! He didn't like to think of what might happen to Sally. . . . Then he saw that she had lifted her head and was staring at him with wide, contemptuous eyes, and she didn't want his sympathy. Between set teeth, she said, "I believed in you—believed you were going to help me rescue my father. And I find you making love to this—"

But Madelon silenced her with a vicious slap and turned furiously on Pete. "You try to trick me, do you? It was not my kisses you wanted, but my gun!"

Pete grinned at her venom. "Sure, you—you swamp bum. Would a man want to kiss you for any other reason?"

Her face white, the Cajun queen spat at him. "You will remember that when you are feeding the 'gators . . . along with this little snip and her father!"

There came a moan from the doorway and the woman turned. "Etienne!" she cried.

And Pete saw, stumbling into the cabin, the fellow whose head he had bashed with his gun before entering to deal with Madelon. She saw her henchman's bloody head and her eyes narrowed with hate as she heard his explanation.

"So the imposter tricked you, as well as Pierre! Now you will have your revenge—you two. You will take his girl"—she glared her hate at Sally—"and . . . we will see how he likes her when you have done with her."

Pierre tightened his brawny arm about Sally's waist and his bearded face bent to hers with that gloating expression Pete had seen back there when he surprised them with the shotgun. He started toward Pierre, but the Cajun woman's automatic suddenly was jammed into his belly.

"*Non, non. . . .*" she purred. "You despise my kisses, do you? Maybe you will like hers better . . . after this!"

And the next instant, the huge fist of Pierre Valois shot over Madelon's shoulder and smacked against Pete's jaw. Almost out, he felt himself sag and drop to the floor, knew that he was being

(Continued on page 120)

His eyes were blood-shot, his expression bestial.

By HARLEY L. COURT

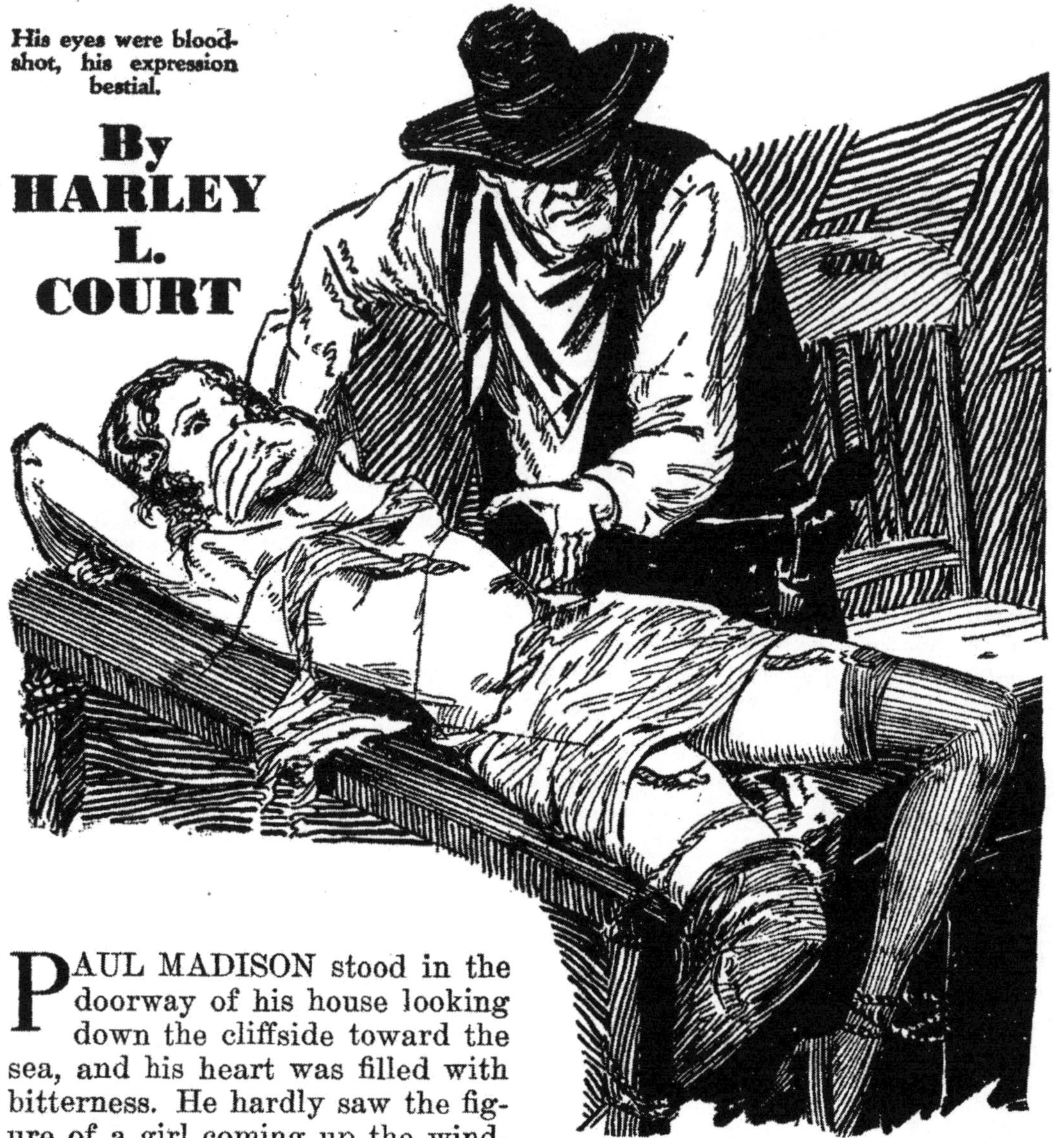

PAUL MADISON stood in the doorway of his house looking down the cliffside toward the sea, and his heart was filled with bitterness. He hardly saw the figure of a girl coming up the winding, rocky path, though, were his thoughts less preoccupied with his own troubles, he could scarcely have failed to notice her, for she ran and stumbled and picked herself up and continued to run breathlessly as if she were pursued.

Madison's thoughts were of himself, of himself as he had been when he had been Captain Madison with a ship under his command. And broodingly he was contrasting that time with the present, with himself, stripped of his command, disgraced, of little more consequence than a piece of driftwood on the beach below.

Then the girl came over the top of the cliff and Madison had to see her. The wind plastered her dress to nubile curves, forcing into prominence the rounded delights of her breast and the clean sweep of her hips and thighs.

Rain had started to fall and Madison took a step forward to meet her. With her wind-blown hair and the lithe grace of her running she was a creature of unusual beauty. And to Madison who had

DIAMONDS UNDER THE SEA

His ship and a fortune in jewels lay fathoms deep. The girl who had risked her life to save him was now a prisoner. How could Captain Madison make his come-back against such tremendous odds?

been looking down on the sea and beach he had loved so well and thinking of them as constituting the graveyard of his career, it was almost as if the grave had opened to bring forth new hope and courage and new life.

He stood to one side and let her pass him into the house. His eyes were quick to note the sharp surging of her breasts beneath wet clinging silk but he said nothing.

She studied him an instant from large brown eyes.

"Captain Madison?"

He shook his head slowly. "No. Just Paul Madison."

She caught at the lapels of his blue coat. "But you were master of the *Avatar?*"

He smiled wearily. "I *was.*"

"Listen, I'm June Holland. You don't know me and probably never will see me again, but you *must* listen to me!"

Madison raised his eyebrows.

"Listen!" The girl's words came in a gush. "Simon French is coming here to force you to go back to the wreck of the *Avatar*. When he has made you do what he wants, he will kill you."

For the first time in a long while Madison displayed some of the forcefulness of character that had brought him, still a young man, to a command on the sea. His fingers bit into the girl's shoulder. A swift savagery came into his voice. "Simon French! What do you know of him—and of me?"

"I know the whole story. I know he was first mate on your ship when it was wrecked. I know that he—not you—was really responsible for running onto the reef."

INTO Madison's mind's eye came a vision of the sturdy little freighter *Avatar,* the ship that now lay under twenty-five fathoms of blue water off Santos Point. His muscles stiffened, and his jaw corded.

"You seem to know a whole lot," he commented bitterly.

The girl went on. "You were bringing a load of lumber from Honduras. You picked up a passenger at San Salvador, a man named Geist. He gave you a package to put in the ship's safe, Captain Madison. But you never put it in the safe."

Madison's eyes fell.

The girl's voice rose. "Did you know what was in that package?"

Madison shook his head, still not looking her in the eye.

"Well, I'll tell you. There was a fortune in diamonds. Geist was a salesman for a European gem dealer. He planned to steal the stones—steal them from his firm and himself. And he bribed Simon French to help him. You were to be the goat."

"How?"

"It was easy. When the *Avatar* went on the reef, it was Simon French's watch. And he piled the ship up deliberately. Then he went down to your cabin, slugged you unconscious while you slept. Together he and Geist slopped liquor all over you, saturated your clothes. They planned to crack the safe open before the ship went down. But the ship was worse damaged than they thought.

"They soon realized they would never get the safe open in time. So they lowered lifeboats and took you off with the rest of the crew. At the examination before the board of inquiry every man on the *Avatar* testified you had been dead drunk when the ship went down. You were dishonorably discharged and your master's license was revoked."

"The diamonds?"

"Geist and French went back to Santos Point in an ocean-going tug. With the aid of divers they got the ship's safe open, and found the stones gone. They knew you hadn't taken them off the *Avatar*. And, therefore, they must still be hidden somewhere on the wreck. Now they plan to shanghai you and take you back to Santos Point. When you've helped them get the diamonds, they intend to kill you."

Madison scratched his head.

"It's a great story, Miss Holland. How do you happen to know all these things?"

"Last night in San Diego in my hotel room I heard voices next door. I listened. It was Geist and French, making plans." She caught Madison's lapels again. "Don't let them find you. Go away before it's too late!"

"No! I guess I'm just not gaited that way. I think I'll wait to talk to Mr. French."

"But you *must* go. They're desperate."

Paul Madison studied her with a fresh interest. This girl had taken much trouble and risked a lot to bring him her warning. His eyes ran over the youthful charm of her slenderness, quickened to her vibrant girlishness. A girl like this could mean much in his disillusioned life. He felt a stirring in his pulses.

And then there came a crunch of tires and a sound of brakes on the landward side of his house.

June Holland paled.

BEFORE Madison could get to the door, there sounded a battering as if a log were being rammed against the frail woodwork. The door wasn't locked but the intruders hadn't paused to discover this fact.

June Holland gasped and fairly flew into the adjoining room. Paul Madison stood grimly in the center of the room as the door sagged inward.

Four men burst into the small bungalow. First, was Simon French, tall, muscular, much scarred. At his heels was the apelike Geist. Two seaman brought up the rear.

The gun in French's hand was menacing.

"Hold it, *captain!*" French ordered sarcastically.

Madison was white with rage but his mind was cool. He realized suddenly that it was essential to the plans of these men that he live! If they killed him now, their fortune in diamonds was lost!

Heedless of the gun, he charged. French's gun-arm came up and chopped down. Madison caught the blow on his left fore-arm and swung from his boot-tops with his right. His former first officer staggered back.

The momentum of Madison's charge carried him on toward Geist and the seamen. He swung again viciously, though his left arm was going numb from the blow from French's gun. One seaman went down. He wouldn't get up in a hurry.

Now he was against the wall by the mantel and he grinned without humor as he remembered the ancient cutlasses that hung there as decorations. He reached backward over his head and dislodged one that fell to the floor. But his hand found the grip on the other.

Geist leaped backward with an oath. Madison rushed him. A movement at the side sent him spinning in a pivot to face the other seaman, who had retrieved the fallen cutlass.

Steel against steel, they thrust and hacked. Sweat ran down Madison's face. The man had the strength of a bull and he used the weapon with skill. For a moment there was silence except for the clash of their blades and the sound of hoarse breathing.

Abruptly Madison changed his tactics with a slashing sweep that terminated in a deceptive feint. The sailor whipped his blade sidewise to counter and Madison brought up his reversed blade to the man's throat. The antique blade slid through flesh and muscle in a spurting of blood.

Madison whirled again, the tip of his blade dripping red.

Simon French snarled and his finger closed on his trigger.

Geist's fist struck the gun as it exploded. "You fool!" he cried. "We must take him alive!" The bullet spatted harmlessly into the floor.

"You'll take nobody—dead or alive!" Madison looked up and saw June Holland in the doorway to his bedroom. A small automatic in her hand covered the first mate, French. "Drop that gun!"

French's gun lowered. But at that instant two swarthy hands reached from in back of the girl and closed on her throat. A one-eyed Mexican had come in through the bedroom window in time to save his masters. June fought desperately to break his hold but he was too strong. His mauling was too much for Madison. Ignoring his other opponents, he leaped to the girl's aid.

French and Geist closed in then. Something heavy came down on Madison's head. He fought for consciousness, but went down under a rain of following blows.

WHEN he came to, he was bound and helpless. He could have been out only a few seconds for the girl still struggled in the grip of Geist and the Mexican. Her dress had been ripped to tatters and her flimsy underthings were poor concealment for her glorious feminine charms.

The one-eyed Mexican licked his lips. His eyes were bestial as he helped Geist tie her wrists behind her.

French grinned as he slid his gaze over the half-naked girl. "You like her, Jose? We'll take her with us."

"Why?" Geist demanded sharply. "She knows too much. She'll only make trouble. Better stick a knife in her here."

French vetoed the suggestion quickly. "What's your hurry? We can get rid of her later. We may be some time down on Santos Point, without any recreation. We'll toss her to the sharks when we've finished."

Bound as he was, Paul Madison managed to get to his feet. He started in a hobbled frenzy toward his enemies, mouthing his hatred. Once more he went down under a volley of kicks and blows. . . .

WHEN next he opened his eyes, night had settled down. His nostrils tingled to the tang of salt sea air. He felt the throbbing of a ship's engines under him and he was conscious of a pitching and tossing that must have come from open water.

He peered about him and discovered himself tied up in a narrow bunk in a tiny cabin. A dim lantern, swinging from the opposite wall gave what little light there was.

Not hurrying, but with great thoroughness, Madison tested the cords that bound his wrists and ankles. They were put there with sailor-like efficiency and his struggles against them resulted only in torture to himself.

Even in those first few minutes he was aware that the pitching of the vessel—apparently a sea-going tug—was increasing in intensity as if the sea were getting rapidly rougher. Every now and then the vibrations of the engines would rise to a definite roar as the propeller would be lifted clear of the water on the crest of a swell.

Despairing of accomplishing anything by main force against his bonds, Madison lay back to take more careful stock of his surroundings. His eyes widened as he stared at the opposite bunk. June Holland, the girl who had risked so much to aid him, lay trussed up there! Her clothing had been torn even more than when he had last seen her and entrancing patches of gleaming white skin showed through in a dozen places. The sight of tender, girlish curves brought Paul Madison's heart leaping into his throat. If anything more should happen to her. . . .

She had apparently been watching him for some time for her eyes were open, and now she smiled. "I was so frightened," she said. "I thought you were dead from the beating they gave you."

"I'm all right," Madison whispered, gratitude for her thought of him pouring over him like a warm flood. "But you . . . ? Did they . . . ?"

"They haven't. At least not yet. . . ."

Madison's mind was scheming, planning. "How long have we been at sea?"

"About two hours."

He spoke as if to himself. "Two hours out of San Diego. . . . And a squall blowing up now. . . . We aren't likely to be bothered for a while. . . ."

Twisting in his bunk, he felt an iron stanchion behind him. It was rough and rusty, but it had an edge that was moderately sharp. Setting his jaws grimly, he began working the cords that fettered his wrists up and down over the edge.

Sweat drenched him and the pain in his constricted arms became intense. But the time came when he felt the first strand give way. Doggedly he continued to saw away. His arms and shoulders were on fire. His skin was raw and bleeding, but another strand parted. And another. Suddenly his arms were free.

With the same stubborn patience he set to restoring the circulation in his numbed hands. It was as if needles were being plunged into him with the return of his blood-flow. But in a few minutes he found he could flex his fingers. And then it was only a short time before his ankles too were free.

He stumbled to his feet and held on to the rail of the bunk to accustom himself to the motion of the deck under his feet. A few seconds later he was kneeling beside June Holland, feverishly plucking at the knots that held her.

Gently he rubbed her wrists and ankles, kneading the circulation back into her shoulders, into the velvety calves of her legs. Still weak and cramped, she turned over and a sudden lunge of the vessel threw her into Madison's arms.

He mightn't have dared to do it himself, but Nature had taken a hand. He looked down into her limpid eyes. He felt the vibrant crush of her breasts against his chest. His mouth dropped to her lips, found them soft, moist, parted, waiting. That kiss lasted an eternity.

She clung to him and the thrilling warmth of her naked skin was like a tonic to him. Her sweetness in his nostrils was an intoxicant.

Then her tiny hands were against the muscularity of his chest, pushing him away. "You mustn't!" she moaned.

"But I love you!"

"And I love you, too. That's why we must be patient, why we mustn't spoil everything," she whispered against his ear.

Though exultation raced through his veins, her words had a sobering effect.

Slowly he stood her on her feet. He chose his words carefully: "You're right, of course. First, we must take care of Simon French. By morning we'll be off Santos Point. He and his crew will be thinking of nothing but the diamonds. . . . Somehow, our chance will come."

He kissed her again and put her back on the bunk. He picked up the cords that had tied her and refastened them about her wrists and ankles, but this time he fashioned knots that looked secure yet could be loosened when she wished. Afterward, he returned to his own bunk and rearranged his bonds. Then there was nothing to do but lie back and wait. . . .

THE ocean was smooth and placid when dawn came. The tug ploughed serenely ahead under full draught.

Listening, Paul Madison interpreted to June, one by one, all the sounds from deck that heralded their reaching their destination, stopping their engines, dropping anchor.

They each were tense and waiting when the cabin door opened and the first rays of morning sunlight broke into their prison.

It was the one-eyed Mexican who entered. He glanced at Madison. "Soon you will be taken on deck to do your work," he said. "Me, I come below early to see my leetle lady."

He turned to June's bunk, hands outstretched, eyes bloodshot. His mouth made grunting, slobbering sounds.

Paul Madison leaped, and his expression was awful to see. There was no sound as his sinewy fingers closed about the Mexican's throat. The man clawed futilely while those fingers tightened inexorably. The Mexican's eyes bulged; his face purpled; he went limp under that strangling hold. But still there was no relenting.

There could be no doubt but that the man was dead when Madison lowered him to the deck.

June started to rise but Madison's hand on her shoulder held her. "They're heavily armed," he whispered. "Together, we'd both be captured. I have a plan, but you can help me more if you'll wait here until I call for you."

Reluctantly the girl agreed. Once more the former master of the *Avatar* drank deep of the sweetness of her lips. Her protestations of love still rang in his ears when he turned and strode out on deck.

HE found Simon French and the jeweler's man, Geist, at the rail, bending over a diving suit. They looked up as he came near, hands in his jacket pockets.

He faced them calmly. "I've eliminated your precious Jose from the picture. I thought, in his place, you might need me."

French's face turned black with rage and his hand reached for his automatic but the ape-like Geist came between him and Madison. Something approaching a smile was forced on his face.

"Of course, Captain Madison. We brought you along because we were sure that you, as an intelligent man, would like to throw in your lot with us. You know why we are here? You remember that package I entrusted with you?"

Madison nodded.

Geist went on: "We're convinced that the package is still in the wreck. It's extremely valuable. We thought that you might remember where you'd hidden it and be willing to help us recover it. If you succeed, we would make it worth your while. In your present position. . . ." He shrugged. "After all, you could use a tidy sum of money, now that your command has been taken from you."

Madison's face was expressionless. "Perhaps I've been a fool," he said. "I'll see what I can do."

"Better see that you make no mistakes," French sneered. "You're going down in the diving suit. And remember! While you're twenty-five fathoms deep, we'll be up here with your air-line. Try to double-cross us, and . . ." He gestured with a finger slashing across his throat.

Madison stared at him as if he were beneath contempt. "Don't be a fool, French. It's even-Stephen, and you know it. I try a fast one, and you've got me where you want me. You play tricks on me, and you lose what you want most!" He turned on his heel and started to inspect the diving rig.

WITH Geist's assistance he climbed into the clumsy canvas. Heavy, leaded shoes clamped his feet. Water-tight cuffs gave his hands a detached feeling. The globular helmet with its circular glass plate closed him in. A test of the air-line showed it to be in working order, and he nodded. They helped him to the platform where a section of rail had been removed. He signified he was ready by means of the signal cord and slowly and easily they lowered him into the clear, sparkling water.

Foot after foot he went down and the pressure on his suit increased. Breathing became more difficult, but it was still not painful. He blew to lower the roaring in his ear-drums. It was nearly twenty minutes before he stood on the deck of his old ship, the *Avatar*.

Deep as he was, the sunlight still filtered down through the waters. A wave of nostalgia hit him and he stood stock-still for a minute studying the old familiar scene. A little tug on his signal cord reminded him of the job to be done and that he didn't have forever to do it.

He made his way up the slanting deck toward his old quarters just aft of the bridge. Gaily colored fish swam in and out of portholes and once he felt a chill run down his spine as a dark, gray shadow glided past the cabin door. A shark!

Inside his cabin, he tugged vigorously at the swollen hatch of a locker he had had set in the paneling of the wall. It came away and he found the metal box with its combination lock that he had placed there so long ago in San Salvador. He shook it and thought he felt Geist's heavy little package move inside.

At the same time he knew hope and fear. Both were concerned with this little metal box. He had had it specially constructed years ago. First, there was the outer shell with its burglar-proof lock. Inside was a smaller container, that was supposed to be water-proof. But would it still be water-proof after its long immersion? So much depended on that!

He made ready to leave the cabin but, before he started, he stopped to pick up a long-bladed knife from his old, abandoned gear.

Knife in one hand, tiny safe in the other, he made his way back on deck and signaled to be brought to the surface.

The signal came back: "Have you found it?"

"Yes."

(Continued on page 126)

FREEBOOTER'S

She came swimming through the Florida Straits, and she told a weird story of cruelty and viciousness. If her story were true, there was great wealth to be had by the man who would accompany her back to the island

FOR three days I had lain around in that damn power boat, anchored in the Florida Straits, waiting for John Frugatti. I was so lonely and sore that I was practically talking to myself. It was a lousy racket Frugatti ran anyway, and he had an idea because I'd worked for him so long, I'd be scared to quit.

That's why he had nerve enough to be throwing a party in Havana when he should be out here giving me instructions about the load I was now hauling. I lay on my back on deck and cursed Frugatti. Once this present load was landed, I was quitting. I did the work and he got the dough! But then I cooled down a little and had to laugh at myself. Quit! How could I quit? For one thing, I owed the boss more money than I was likely to see in a month of Sundays. In the second place, there wasn't a town along the coast that wasn't looking for me. You can't spend a year and a half smuggling without your description getting out.

Even in Mexico and in Cuba they didn't want me. Money'll fix almost any rap, but it would take a bale of jack to put me in the clear.

While I lay there, trying to dope some sort of an out for myself, the sun had already begun to go down. The water around my boat sparkled like gold. I never yet have got tired of seeing one of those Florida sunsets. I got up and went to the side.

A moving flash of black and white caught my eye, gliding toward the boat about thirty or forty feet away. A shark! I stepped into the cabin, came out with my rifle. I had no particular desire to kill, but it gave me something to do.

My sights were lined when the thing turned on its back in the tinted water and there was a gleam of white flesh that no fish could have made. I put down the gun and could hardly believe my eyes. My shark was a woman! But it couldn't be!

My boat, the *Trixie,* was anchored at least fifty miles southeast of Key West. The Salt Keys lay in the opposite direction, at almost the same distance. The mainland was another twenty miles away. Of course, she could have come from some millionaire playboy's yacht that was cruising these waters. I knew the kind of parties those guys were all the time throwing. Maybe somebody'd got too rough and she was walking home from the ride!

But it didn't add up. Probably my business had taught me to be suspicious. I turned from the girl and squinted around the horizon. There was always the chance that it was a trick, that she was a decoy from a coast guard boat.

CACHE

By GEORGE DRAKE

Except for her utter weariness she seemed all right.

Satisfied that there was no other boat around, I gave my attention to the swimmer again. She was near enough now so that I could see she was very tired, in spite of her tapered legs and muscled calves like those of a professional dancer.

She reached weakly for a dangling rope and the motion brought into high relief the mounds of her rounded breasts. Her hips had a flare that was all woman—that made me think of parties with good liquor, good food, good music, and women that were good for parties anyway.

I helped her on deck and her eyes thanked me, even as she went limp in my arms. I thought it was a gag for a second, but then I knew she had fainted. Exhaustion, I guess.

FOR a minute or two I held her, marveling at the beauty of her slender white body. She wore a man's shorts and a man's tattered polo shirt, much too small for the glorious loveliness of her rising and falling breasts. Spent as she was, she literally gasped for air, emphasizing every nuance of her bosom with her rhythmic breathing. My brain ran riot, both from my admiration of her superb figure, and from the curiosity that devoured me.

We were miles and miles from land, and yet she had come nonchalantly out of the sunset waters like a mermaid! It was too much for me!

I swung her up in my arms and carried her below, to my own bunk. Except for her utter weariness, she seemed perfectly all right. She lay there, red lips parted, and I couldn't resist the impulse. I bent my mouth to hers, felt its soft fullness, tasted its sweetness. And she stirred beneath my caress and her hands went fluttering to my shoulders. I kissed her again. This time her eyelids lifted slowly. Through veiling lashes I glimpsed the blue of cornflowers.

She tried to sit up, pushing me away gently in the act.

"I'm so tired," she murmured, and sank back on the pillow.

I could thing of nothing to say. I'm afraid my words were stupid at the moment. "Been swimming long?"

"Since about noon."

Half an hour later she was sitting up, with a blanket drawn around her shoulders, drinking the coffee I had prepared for her. And for ten minutes I had been listening wonderingly to her story.

She finished, and I shook my head. "You certainly got a break when I happened to be anchored right here. You must have had at least a ten mile swim. If the *Trixie* weren't here, you could have gone right on to Ireland without meeting anybody!"

She shuddered and the blanket skidded on one gleaming, rounded shoulder. She clutched it together tightly so that it followed the contours of her figure, and I could feel a little pulse hammering at my temple.

But I was still thinking of what she had told me. "I've heard of Eden Island. Only it used to be Mack's Mistake. That's where old Stanley Mack started his colony, dedicated to the brotherhood of man."

"Yes," she said. "I am Stanley Mack's granddaughter, Hope. I *had* to get away from the island. Even if I hadn't found you—if it meant swimming until I couldn't swim any more and was drowned, it would have been better than staying there." Her voice speeded with excitement.

"In the last month there's been murder on Eden Island—not one murder, but half a dozen. What's more, my grandfather is dying by inches—killed by his no-good, Cuban wife and her sweetheart. Look!"

She leaped to her feet on the floor of the cabin and, turning her back to me, let the blanket fall to her waist. With a quick jerk she pulled the polo shirt up to her neck, revealing an expanse of sun-tanned skin that was criss-crossed with vicious welts.

"Do you know what those marks are?" she demanded bitterly. "Whip marks. Most every woman on Eden Island has scars like that. In most cases, their husbands have been killed in cold blood. It's supposed to be a form of punishment, but really it's just an attempt to beat us all into submission."

"Why hasn't there been an investigation?"

"Who'd bother to investigate? My grandfather bought the island outright when he started the colony. There were two dozen of us who came down, twelve men and twelve women. As soon as our stores and supplies were safely landed, we burned our boats. Arrangements were made for a Danish steamer to stop every six months with fresh supplies. But all this that has been happening has taken place in the last few weeks. It all began with my grandfather's Cuban wife and her affair with Batista. The beatings and the murders started with that."

IN SPITE of the whip-lashes on the girl's back, I found it hard to believe her. This was like something out of a book of fiction. Like her crack-brained old grandfather, the girl must be a little touched in the head. But I decided to humor her.

"What can I do to help you?"

"Take me to Key West. Your boat is fast. We can make it in a few hours. Then I'll get help and go back. I tell you my grandfather is dying by inches from the poison they have given him."

There was hysteria in her eyes, in her tone, in the excited, vibrant palpitation of her breasts. I felt sorry for her.

I laughed but without mirth. "Unfortunately I can't show my face in Key West. In a pinch I could run you to Cardenas, or up to the Banks north of here. But I'm in no position to get mixed up in your affairs."

She had the polo shirt back in place now. She turned about and her eyes searched my face. "You mean you're afraid to get tangled up with the law?" There was scorn in her words.

"That's my business! All you need to know is that I'm not putting this boat into Key West!"

Her scrutiny of me narrowed shrewdly. "If you're smuggling, breaking the law in any way, maybe you *have* a little nerve. Would you like to try your luck without the help of the authorities? There's more money mixed up in this business than you could make in a year running Chinamen! You've got a rifle, and there isn't a gun on the island. Help me get my grandfather and I'll show you more treasure than your boat will hold."

I laughed shortly. "Wasn't your story wild enough without the treasure angle?" I asked her.

She blazed. "You're yellow! Coward! You're afraid!" She was magnificent, standing white and erect only inches away from me.

I did the normal thing. I reached out my arms and drew her to me. Her lithe, only half-covered body in my embrace was intoxicating. She fought; kicked; hammered at me with little fists; but I had been too much alone for a long time. I crushed her until I could feel her heartbeats under the cushioned softness against my chest. I bruised her mouth on my own, heedless of her frenzied struggles. The feel and sight of her supple loveliness was something that I couldn't have resisted to save my soul. . . .

LATER I was at the wheel on deck and a cool, fresh breeze was washing my face. Curiously, instead of feeling exultation, I was possessed by a sense of shame. I had started the boat's motor, not knowing what I intended to do. I wasn't in doubt long.

I felt a prodding in the small of my back. Then Hope Mack's voice came, small but determined. "That's your rifle that you feel. Don't make me shoot it. You're setting a course for Eden Island."

Maybe I'd intended to do that anyway. Now the choice was out of my hands. I shrugged and obeyed. There was silence for fifteen minutes.

I spoke before she did. "I wish you'd put that gun down," I told her. "You make me nervous. I'm not going to do anything but what you tell me. You want your damned island. You're going to get it! As for the rifle, I've got a gun here in my shirt and could have shot you almost any time in the last fifteen minutes."

She gasped.

"You see I didn't," I assured her. "Your story sounds wacky to me, but I admire your nerve. Maybe I'm trying to help you because I feel sort of like a heel, myself. In any case, you need rest now. Lie down and take a nap. I'll call you as soon as I raise Eden Island."

She stretched out on a low locker on deck and I thought I heard muffled sobbing before there came the more measured whisper of her sleeping breaths. I looked over my shoulder and admired her in the moonlight. The gun was beside her where she lay, the blanket half over her. There was a suggestion of the gleam of tears on her eyelashes. In her complete relaxation, she was no longer the angry woman but much more like a tired child. I slipped the throttle forward another notch and we picked up speed.

THE dark mass against the skyline that was Eden Island was only a few hundred yards ahead when I awakened her. She shivered under the gentle insistence of my hands on her shoulders. "We're here," I said. "What comes next?"

"You mean you've changed your mind? You're going to help me?"

"Why not? I'm probably a screwball, but what the hell! I was just killing time anyway."

Then she was on her feet, swaying toward me. I could feel the light touch of her hands. In the moonlight her lips were tremulous. "I'm so glad!" she whispered. "I promise you you'll never be sorry. There's a little creek a short distance to the right. Head up it slowly."

Twenty minutes later we were on dry land. A small area had been cleared back from the beach and I could make out the shapes of a group of palm-thatched huts. Two stood apart from the others. There were probably half a dozen of them.

Lights showed only in the windows of the two that were by themselves. They were larger than those grouped in darkness. Hope took my hand and led me noiselessly through the shadows toward the lighted huts.

Moonlight came through in silvery patches, patches that flickered as the light breeze stirred the palms. Behind us I could hear the monotonous ripple of surf on the beach. All my senses were unusually alert, and I carried my rifle as if it were dynamite.

We stopped a few feet from the first of the huts to peer into the dimly lighted room. From our angle we could see nothing but a far corner of the room where an old man lay on an untended cot. His beard was long and white, his figure thin to the point of emaciation. It could be no one but Stanley Mack, founder of the ill-fated colony.

Looking at him, half covered by a dirty blanket, his mild blue eyes glowing with a vacant stare, it was hard to remember that this man had been a millionaire before the days of Eden Island—or Mack's Mistake. His ribs were as prominent as those of an umbrella; his long hair and beard matted and uncared for. Over and over in a childish monotone he quoted scripture, evidently to himself.

I gripped my rifle more firmly, patted Hope's shoulder in sympathy, and crept closer to the window. Now I could see the other figure in the room.

She sat without motion in an upright chair, watching the poor, insane old man. Between the two of them was a table littered with dirty dishes. I could tell little beyond the fact that she was a woman for she was garbed in a long tan robe with a hood that concealed most of her face in shadows.

Hope caught my wrist and drew me away. "It's grandfather's Cuban wife," she whispered. "We'll wait until she goes to Batista, her lover. Then we'll follow."

Nodding acquiesence, I stole after the girl to the second of the isolated huts. As long as I live, I'll never forget the scene that confronted us there. Half sitting, half lying, on a homemade couch was one of the most gigantic men I've ever seen. His nude, almost coffee-colored torso glistened with sweat. And all around him were the women of the colony, his harem.

ONE stood behind him and fanned him with a fan made of palm fronds. At his feet crouched another white woman, apparently his plaything of the moment. Her whole attitude was one of abject terror. Half a dozen women garbed in various states of deshabille hugged the far walls. On each of their faces was a look of mingled fear and loathing.

Batista grunted and gestured. The nearest of the other women poured liquor into his glass from a huge jug, then backed away, trembling.

Hope pressed my fingers. "Anne and Mary are gone," she whispered. "He must have taken them to the whipping cave for punishment."

I would have questioned her but just then the door opened and the tan-gowned Cuban woman entered from the other side of the hovel. Now the lamp-light was full on her face and I had an opportunity to study her. There was a gleam in her eyes like coals from a fire. Otherwise her face was placid except for the crimson slash of her mouth which now was grim with anger.

Batista found his feet and bowed insolently. At the foot of the couch the cringing woman did not move. I might have thought her dead but for the labored rise and fall of her rounded breasts.

The Cuban woman's lips drew back in a snarl and I knew that a turbulent scene was in prospect, but Hope drew me away before I had a chance to witness more. "This is our chance to get grandfather," she murmured. "Hurry!"

We made for the other hut, only to discover a hazard we had not noticed before. Still mouthing scripture, old Stanley Mack sat up in bed at our appearance, but otherwise paid us no more attention than the dishes on the table. I started to help him to his feet when I uncovered the obstacle that we had overlooked. A heavy steel chain fettered one bony ankle to a ring in the wall of the place!

For the time being we were helpless. I had no idea what to do. The girl made one forlorn suggestion. She would go back to Batista's hut as if she had been roaming around the island all day. While he and the Cuban woman bickered, she might be able to steal the key.

I didn't like the idea, but I had nothing better to offer. Hope pressed a hasty kiss on my mouth as if in forgiveness for my actions on the *Trixie* and left me.

THEN began the interminable wait. With my rifle across my knees, ready for instant action, I sat there in the shadows while time droned on. My nerves were on edge but I was afraid that any move I might make could easily ruin everything. Even the lapping of the waves on the sandy beach and the constant sough of the wind through the palms had an eerie quality. Night birds called and insects buzzed, and still I waited, tensed nearly to the breaking-point.

All this time my imagination was full of ugly conjecture. I had too clear a vision of what I had seen through Batista's window ever to tolerate for an instant the thought of Hope Mack in his bestial arms.

Now, it seemed to me, there could be but one explanation of the girl's long delay. Something had gone wrong with her plans, there in the hut. Once I had decided that, it was a matter of seconds before I was back at that lighted window.

The crouching woman at the foot of the couch still huddled there. Her full bosom still lifted and fell with her agitated breathing. The woman with the fan still waved it. The half dozen others still cowered by the wall. At the table in the center of the room, Stanley Mack's Cuban wife sat, grim and implacable, glaring at the other women colonists. Otherwise the room was empty. Hope and Batista were gone!

For once I decided the time for direct action had come. I strode swiftly around the building to its entrance. My rifle was held meaningfully when I stepped into the doorway.

"Where's Hope?" I demanded.

If I had thought my surprise appearance was going to startle them into blurting out the truth, I was far wrong. Only the tan-gowned Cuban paid any attention to me.

She, without showing the slightest emotion, pivoted slowly in her chair and fixed me with her burning gaze. I said, "Listen!" and swung the gun into line.

She remained stolid. I took a step forward and was warned by the tiniest, inoluntary flicker from one of the other women's eyes. I dove for the floor, rolling as I fell.

Batista, grin still on his face, stood there, slightly off balance from his vicious machete blow that I had barely escaped.

Automatically I brought up the rifle and fired. The big man hesitated, jerked as if slapped, then toppled. His Cuban sweetheart took that moment to tip over the lamp. There were screams from the others.

A ghost-like form glided past me toward the door. I grabbed instinctively, and for a few seconds wrestled with a form that bit and kicked and scratched and gouged. My fingers closed on a soft throat as one of the women relit the lamp with trembling hands.

Beneath me was the spitting figure of old man Mack's tawny skinned wife. But there was no sign of Batista. Except for a damp splotch on the floor where he had fallen, there was no indication that he had been in the hut at all.

I dragged the tan-robed Cuban to her feet. I slapped her across the vicious gash of her mouth, and I put real stinging power into my slap. My blood was boiling. "You've had all but your last chance," I snarled. "Where is Hope—before I kill you?"

Her face twisted sarcastically but she displayed no fear.

It was the woman on the couch who came to my rescue. "The cave! The cave! That's where he took her! And he'll kill her if you don't save her in time!"

My mind was in a turmoil, and I found it hard to think clearly. This whole thing was like a mad nightmare, nowhere touching upon reality. Yet the thought of Hope's sweet, white loveliness in the pawing hands of that beast spurred me to action.

WITH alternate proddings from my toe and the rifle I spun the Cuban woman out the door. "I'm going to the cave," I said grimly. "And you're showing me the way. One little trick from you, and I'm going to start marking you up. Maybe you aren't afraid of being killed. I don't intend to kill you. But, cross me, and I'll leave you the sort of cripple that will make children scream if they see you!"

Reluctantly she started off into the darkness.

While we walked, I took the shells from my rifle and threw the weapon far to one side in the underbrush. Automatic in hand I followed the tan-robed woman. At places we seemed to be following a path bordered with low-growing shrubbery. At times we crossed trackless expanses of sand. But now that we were on our way, we didn't hesitate or falter.

Only once I permitted her a few seconds to rest.

She eyed me carelessly. "Who are you?"

"What's it to you?"

"A policeman?"

"Perhaps. It can't matter to you. All that you need to know is that I'm in charge now. You do as I say. Get going!"

She stumbled on, but more slowly than before. She must have been turning things over in her mind, for suddenly she spoke over her shoulder:

"I'll take you to the cave on one condition. The next time that you see Batista, don't miss. Kill him!"

I had never encountered anything more cold-blooded in my life—and I'd been used to dealing with conscienceless criminals. It nauseated me. But I thought I understood the idea behind her words.

"I see," I said. "You want your lover put out of the way so that he can't blab about your other killings. If it means anything to you, I have no connection with the law. Take me to Hope Mack before it is too late and you can rub out half the population of the Antilles, for all I care."

She stopped short and scrutinized my face, oblivious to my shoves and proddings to go on. Her eyes held me magnetically and I began to feel more and more perturbed. But she wouldn't budge until she had made up her mind.

Abruptly the hard gleam softened in her gaze.

"I understand," she murmured softly. "You're in love with that undeveloped child. You fool!"

She shrugged and her austere robe slid from her shoulders. She stood there as motionless as if carved in stone. The moonlight bathed her proud arrogance, bringing out gloriously every subtle line of her flimsily clad figure. Her breasts were round and firm, shaped as if by an inspired sculptor. Her waist was flat and slender, swelling miraculously into hips that were the epitome of feminine enticement. Long, slender, straight legs drew my attention, and I traced their length from her superb thighs, down perfect calves, tapering into perfect ankles.

I loathed the woman for her viciousness but, nevertheless, I could feel the heat of my blood as it coursed riotously through my veins. In the silvery moonlight her skin had the sleekness and texture of polished ivory.

"Make up your mind," she purred. "Do you still love that child when there are women like me to know?"

Her bringing Hope back into my mind broke her evil spell at least temporarily. "Quit stalling for time!" I snapped. "Pull your robe back on. I'm not interested in anybody but Hope."

"You're a fool," she told me, as she turned to lead the way. "If the beauty of a woman like me means nothing to you, what about money? Does gold interest you? More wealth than you ever dreamed of? Listen! I can show you more gold than you could possibly ever spend. Kill Batista, and you may load your boat with it."

I might have listened to her at another time. Now my thoughts were all on Hope. "Shut up!" I told the Cuban. "If Batista has harmed Hope, I'll tear him apart. If he hasn't, we'll see what happens."

WE WALKED on in absolute silence, but my mind was still turning over what she had said. First, Hope had talked of treasure.

Now, this woman. And then, strangely, my thoughts went back to my brooding on the *Trixie* just before Hope had come swimming out. If I had money enough, I could square myself with the law. I could quit the rackets and live respectably, a free man.

The Cuban woman must have been a mind-reader. She paused again, came up to me, thrust a coin in my hand. "Will you believe me now?" she asked.

The coin was surprisingly heavy. I turned it over in my hand. It was a gold doubloon, an old Spanish piece o' eight!

"So that's it!" I cried. "Pirate loot! Now I see the motive behind all these killings!"

Her laugh carried an evil ring. Her eyes were greedy. "Smart boy!" she said. "Since we came here, we've discovered a pirate's cache. Instead of dividing it a dozen or more ways, we've—" She drew a slim finger across her neck suggestively and I shuddered. "Now," she went on, "you kill Batista and there will be only the two of us to worry about. We'll share the treasure equally."

I didn't answer and I think she thought she had me convinced. She started off again, much more rapidly, and I trudged after her, drenched with perspiration. A little farther on the trail took an upward turn and soon we were making our way along the side of a rocky cliff.

We turned a bend and the forbidding black entrance of a cave loomed before us. She took a torch from a crevice in the rocky wall and thrust it into my hand. I lit it and followed her down an inky passageway into a sort of vaulted chamber. Its floor was littered with the ashes of many fires.

She reached for the torch and stuck it into a niche, gesturing as she did so to a fissure in the rock beside her. I leaned forward, trembling with excitement, to look. A huge brass-bound trunk, its lid thrown back, had been hidden there. It was heaped with coins, so many that they had spilled over the sides. Even in the shadow I was certain that they were doubloons.

Her hand touched my arm. I turned and she was very close. "They're ours. Yours and mine—together," she breathed. Again the robe was slipping from her shoulders.

Fascinated, I saw her for the second time, slender and shapely, possessing in one body all the allure that woman has held since the beginning of time. "All you have to do is kill Batista," she whispered. Her dark eyes were blazing, her breasts palpitating with excitement. "Kill Batista, and you may have the gold—*and me!*" She came so close that I could feel her animal warmth, fancied I could hear the beating of her heart, were not mine pounding so loudly.

"Bring the gold out into the light," she told me. "Look at it. Feel it. Try to realize what it can mean to you!"

As if in her spell, I put my gun aside. I grasped a handle of the heavy chest, pulling and tugging. Then her laughter rang out and I was sane again. I leaped to the rock where I had put my automatic, but I was too late.

She held the gun familiarly,

trained steadily at my middle. "You fool!" she cried. "Stand back. You no longer will have the gold, nor will you have me! And you won't kill Batista!"

She gestured to the torch and I had no choice but to pick it up. "Straight ahead," she ordered.

The passageway into which we passed was narrower than the last but soon it began to broaden and I sensed we were entering another natural chamber. She urged me on.

This second chamber was as large as the first and it was lighted by a dozen or more torches. At the far end as we entered I could see the drooping forms of two women, tied by their wrists to spikes in the rocky wall far over their heads. There backs were hideous with raw welts, dried and clotted blood.

Anxiously I peered about for Hope but for a moment couldn't see her. I glimpsed Batista moving toward me from one side but my eyes were seeking the girl I loved.

I didn't even have a chance to duck. Something heavy in the big man's hand came down on my skull. I pitched forward, unconscious before I hit the floor.

VOICES, loud and angry, brought me back to earth. For a moment I made no effort to open my eyes. I realized that my wrists were bound and that I was lying on hard rock. I listened.

Batista's voice came first. "I am tired of you," he cried. "I am still a young man, but you are old. Soon your beauty will all be gone. I want a young woman—not one like you!"

"You are very stupid," the Cuban woman taunted him. "You bring her here to torture her—to find out where she has been. And she works on you, talks you into this! It's all part of her plan to make trouble between us. You're a woman-crazy fool, Batista, or you could see that."

I opened my eyes a crack. Batista and the woman faced each other only a few feet away. Batista had his left arm around Hope Mack's shoulders, his other held a wicked-looking machete. Hope entered the argument now.

"Don't believe the old witch, Batista. You know I love you. What do you want of an old woman like her?"

The Cuban woman's eyes were afire with jealous rage. She lifted my automatic but Batista was before her. The machete in his hand darted venomously. Blood spurted from the Cuban's cheek and stained her robe. She staggered backward as Batista lunged again.

Then everything happened at once. I was aware of Hope kneeling beside me, working at the cords that bound me. My wrists came free just as the gun in the woman's hand exploded. Even as he fell, Batista slashed out twice.

The two of them went to the floor together, to sprawl side by side, as if preparing to sleep.

Stupefied by the suddenness of it all, I stared down at them. Hope crept into the circle of my arm, sobbing with relief.

"I thought you'd never find me," she cried. "I had to make believe with Batista to gain more time. I wonder if I'll ever feel clean again."

BEFORE night came again, the *Trixie* was at sea, headed for Key West. Below were the women colonists who would have another chance to live. With them was a sick old man, muttering from the scriptures. And in the same cabin was a squat, brass-bound chest of gold doubloons.

I stood on deck, whistling into the breeze. My right hand held the wheel. My left arm was about Hope's shoulders. All that had happened was past now. Before us I could see nothing but a glamorous future.

Never-Never Corpses

[Continued from page 17]

"By God!" Walton whispered. "Listen!"

ANOTHER scream had sounded; this time from the throat of a man—a black man. The sound was hideous, as if ripped out of death's own yawning jaws. Then there was a shout. Another wild, gibbering yell. Footfalls pounded.

And at that instant, an orange disc of moon slid up over the far, serrated mountain-range. It cast yellow illumination over the earth below. Through that stained and watery light came movement—flitting, racing black figures.

Trenlawn's abbos and lubras, driven like harried animals by another ebony shape which was Bill-Big-Ears!

Bill had a spear, and its tip glistened wetly in the moonlight. Walton suddenly knew the meaning of that hideous death-yell he'd just heard. The spearpoint had tasted kidney fat!

Two of the abbos bore Lisbeth between them, dragging her along as they raced for safety. Her nightgown and her negligee had been ripped, torn from her shoulders. The upper slopes of her breasts gleamed yielding-white in the moonglow; her bare, kicking legs lashed desperately at her captors. Behind them, Bill-Big-Ears paused, stopped, raised his left hand. His fingers were clenched around a curved wooden boomerang. He hurled it.

The deadly wooden thing sailed forward; crushed the skull of one of Lisbeth's kidnapers. The man went down without a sound. His companion released his hold on Lisbeth's other arm and dived wildly toward a clump of gum.

Walton swung his gun into line; triggered it. His slug slammed into the running bushman's leg, knocked him down. Now there were but two remaining abbos and a thin cluster of bare-breasted, wailing lubras. Walton fired over their heads; halted them as Bill-Big-Ears sprinted up.

Hold um fella black boys with your spear, Bill!" the police corporal yelled. "Herd 'em together. Good boy!" Then he whirled on Trenlawn. "Now, then, mister. Hold out your wrists for the irons."

Trenlawn said: "Like hell!" and smashed himself at Walton.

Walton grinned. Deliberately he holstered his gun. "I've wanted this chance for quite a number of hours, mister," he said. He crouched, set his legs wide apart, balled his fists. "Come on."

"I'm coming, tin soldier." Trenlawn's charge was like the rush of an infuriated 'roo. He leaped to battle in long, loping strides, and his moondrenched face was a mask of hatred.

Sprawled in the grass, Lisbeth cried: "Ted—look out—he'll kill you—!"

"Not he. He's through killing." Walton parried a roundhouse swing; countered with a jolting, jarring uppercut that rocked his adversary's head far back. And while it was back, the corporal slammed home a left to the heavier man's gullet.

THE blue of sudden cyanosis suffused Trenlawn's cheeks as he choked and strangled, his breathing cut off in his paralyzed throat. Walton struck again, his knuckles smearing Trenlawn's nose to a spongy pulp that spurted crimson.

The murderer backed off, gasping. Walton stepped in for the finish—and walked up against a piledriver right that took him over the heart like the smash of a sledgehammer. His lungs were suddenly afire. His ribs were caved in. Broken, he knew. Several of them. Pain slammed through him like a riptide, rocking him, bleeding the strength out of his legs. He felt himself going down.

He mustn't go down, he told himself. He *couldn't* go down! He had a job to do—a killer to take. He sobbed out in anguish as he forced his body straight. Thumbs reached out, seeking his eyeballs to blind them. He felt the berserk pressure—

With everything he had left, he struck. Struck wildly, without aim, without reason. His fist smashed against the granite of Trenlawn's lantern chin. It was Ted Walton's last blow; he knew that. He had broken his hand. The pain screamed upward through his forearm, into his biceps and his shoulder. He was finished, done. Stolidly, like an ox awaiting slaughter, he waited for Trenlawn to take him.

Trenlawn didn't. Trenlawn's eyes were walled back in their sockets; only the whites were showing. His broken jaw hung limply where the corporal's final, devastating punch had jarred it from its hinges, shattered it. He fell forward, like a tall tree hacked through at the base. He stirred no more.

Then Lisbeth cried a shrill warning. "Ted—behind you—*those abbos—!*"

Stupidly, Walton pivoted. The two wild blacks had broken away from Bill-Big-Ears, while the lubras clawed and scratched at him to impede him. The bushmen, driven to frenzy when they saw their white boss bested, were coming at the policeman in a last vicious effort to kill him so they could escape punishment for having laid hands on Lisbeth.

Walton dragged out his gun. There was one shell left in it. He fired—over the oncoming frizzy heads.

He knew his abbos. They stopped, their teeth chattering in fright. Walton walked slowly toward them, reached them, grabbed them in spite of the fury that raged in his right hand. He banged their skulls together.

They dropped.

"Put um fella black boys in neck-irons—fella white killer too," Walton said to Bill-Big-Ears. Then he faced Lisbeth; took her into his arms. "Let's find your father and tell him all's well," he said.

Her eyes were stars shining. She wanted to be kissed. He kissed her.

Red Eden

[Continued from page 39]

them, with Nigger Jake and Bowers. In the second were Lucas, Fish, and Freddy. The little Sydney trader hadn't come. Fighting wasn't a part of his life, and he was interested only in the copra. He was sitting with old Woo and two other cronies, teaching the Melanesian girl to play poker, and wondering what had become of the other one, the pretty Polynesian.

In the soft splash of the dinghies' oars, nobody had heard a softer splash, or seen a lithe, brown, feminine figure, attired in even less than the customary South Seas garment — which isn't too much—dive from a rock and streak through the phosphorescent waters in the direction of Eden's schooner.

That figure, cleaving the waves like a dolphin, easily outdistanced the cumbrous dinghies as they maneuvered toward Eden's yacht. The plan was to storm her from port and starboard simultaneously. They were trying to keep in touch with each other in the darkness—and Marya was swimming straight toward her objective.

It was a cry from Bembo that first announced to Eden the dripping female figure clambering over the rail. Bembo ran forward with his revolver at Marya's stomach, and then drew back and grinned.

Eden had broken out more than revolvers. He had broken out a bottle of special Scotch, and he was as drunk as he had ever been in his life. He grinned at the girl, and pawed her smooth, sleek, dripping shoulders, rubbery-soft and warm. What the hell did he care about that fool of a woman below?

"So you don't like Pango?"

"I came back to you," said Marya, chuckling.

Eden decided he'd take Marya and go for a cruise through the islands. He had brought Marya to Pango because she had begged him so hard, and she reminded him of the other Marya he'd known. He'd go native, he'd. . . .

"I came back to you, to warn you, Red. Lucas and Marais are coming in a few minutes to get the schooner. Maybe you can see the dinghies out there."

Eden's whirling consciousness

grew instantly calm. Eden had wanted a chance to settle scores with Marais for a long time. It looked as if it was coming now.

"You're a good girl, Marya," he said. He put his arms about the Polynesian girl's sleek body and felt the undulations of her breasts as she leaned against him. "But hell, you've got to have something on," he laughed. "Here, put on this!"

He stripped off his tattered sweater and put it over Marya's head. It had stretched it; came half way down Marya's thighs.

RED EDEN strode down and unlocked the little cabin. Nude to the waist now, and reeling with liquor, he must have appeared a terrific spectacle to Beth. She uttered a shriek, and cowered back against the wall. Eden looked at her in the suit of dungarees, and laughed.

He picked up an old shirt that he had tossed into a corner, and put it about him. "You're a scared little fool," he said, "and Marais and your other friends are coming to try to get this boat and take you back to Pango. God help you if they win! I'm not going to harm you. Can you get that through your head? I don't want you. I've got my native girl aboard. I'm just trying to save you. See?"

"Freddy—Freddy—?" gasped Beth.

"Nobody's likely to harm Freddy, especially if his old man comes across with a few hundred pounds some day. Freddy's ten times as safe as you are—and you haven't the sense to know it."

Red Eden tucked the shirt into his trousers and turned away. He had the key in his hand, and he meant to lock the little fool in the cabin only at that moment an outburst of yells from the deck indicated that the attack had begun.

Eden was up the companion in two bounds. He saw a dim mass of struggling figures on the deck. He heard revolvers cracking. A figure staggered back against him, already dying, blood gushing from the mouth, and in the dimness Eden recognized Bembo.

Bembo killed by those devils? Hell, Eden had always liked Bembo, though Bembo's wife, on one of the outer islands, had always hated him because—well, for the best possible because. Eden went mad. His gun burst flame, and, with a long, shuddering cry, Lucas dropped across his feet, threshed, and was still.

It was Nigger Jake whose slug whizzed past Eden's face. He was half American and half Melanesian, and Eden had never liked Nigger Jake, because he seemed the wrong sort of mongel. Some mongrels are all right, but this blend hadn't been a happy one. Nigger Jake fired again, and Eden felt the sting across his shoulder. Eden fired, and there was no more Nigger Jake—only a face that was blending into an amorphous mass, attached to a sagging, slumping body.

They had George down. They had Marya down, and the shirt that Eden had given her wasn't following the styles. Marais was shrieking with that mixture of blood lust and woman-hunger that, when properly combined, makes men fiends.

IT WAS knives now, because knives are the common weapon of the Islands, and the revolvers were empty. Red Eden didn't need a knife. A good, club-like fist is a better weapon than a knife. Marais, Bowers, and Fish were stabbing at the Kanaka, George, and Marya's brown limbs were flailing, and she was clawing at the three. That was when Eden leaped into action.

A single blow of one of Eden's fists laid Marais prostrate on the deck. Old Bowers, crouching back against the rail, gibbered and mouthed, flourishing the knife impotently in his hand. Fish sprang with a snarl, and Eden swept him overboard with a single movement of his arm.

Eden leaped at Marais, whose knife had fallen from his hand. He picked the Frenchman up in his arms as easily as if he had been a child, and slung him bodily at old Bowers, knocking Bowers backward over the rail likewise.

A bellow of anguish came from Marais' lips. That blow of the rail must have inflicted some frightful internal injury, for the Frenchman's voice was choked with bubbling blood, which streamed from his lips. Somehow, quick as a cat, Marais had eluded Eden and grabbed the knife. He lunged.

The point of the blade ripped through Eden's shirt and gashed his side. A rib deflected it and twisted the weapon out of Marais' hand. And Eden started to beat Marais to pieces.

Eden had many an old grudge against Marais, many a trading score to settle, but it was on account of Beth that he was killing

Marais. He was killing him in the way he knew best, and shriek upon shriek of agony broke from Marais as those pounding fists hammered home upon face and chest and belly. The flopping thing that Eden had propped against the wheelhouse was ceasing to have much resemblance to a human figure. It was literally disintegrating under the blows of Eden's fists.

And even Eden grew appalled at the sight of his own work. He picked the dead thing up in his arms and heaved it over the side.

MARYA was clinging to him, her soft arms about his neck. Eden felt the softness of her breasts against him, and relaxed for a moment after the panting struggle of the slaying. He saw Kanaka George, apparently unharmed, circling about him. On the deck lay the bodies of Lucas and Bembo. Eden wasn't thinking of anybody else, certainly not of Freddy, because Freddy had only been an incident. Freddy had a sort of courage, but he was a weakling at heart; he didn't rank with fighting men.

George knew that Freddy was on the boat, but even George wasn't able to see to the end of it, where Freddy and Beth were crouching in the bow. Beth was whispering, "Kill him now! Kill him now!"

Freddy came gliding forward out of the darkness, a revolver in his hand. "Damn you!" he screamed, as he fired point blank at Eden.

The slug passed between Eden's arm and chest, grazing both. Eden shouted, and then he had Freddy in those great hands of his, and he was fighting down the desire to do to him what he had done to Marais, for Beth's sake.

He tore the revolver from Freddy's hands, and he shook the little Limy like a rat. Freddy, limp in Eden's grasp, didn't whimper or scream. Perhaps that was what saved him. He waited for Red Eden's doom.

"What am I going to do with you, rat?" asked Eden.

Beth screamed, "Let him go! Let us both go! What is it you want? His father will pay you all the money you ask of him!"

Marya had slipped her arm

through Eden's. She was looking from his face to Beth's. She knew that Eden liked this white woman, and she didn't see much chance for herself. Yet she had never really wanted to go to Pango; she had only wanted to be with Eden.

Beth screamed again: "Let him go! Let him go!"

"You think you love him, huh?" gritted Eden. "If you think so, I'll take you both to Sydney—free."

Eden pushed Freddy away and detached himself from Marya, and stood examining Beth's face in the darkness. He couldn't see it very clearly, but he knew that this was the woman he had always wanted. This was almost the same woman for whose sake he had given up being a theological student in a ridiculous little New England town.

BETH, staring back at Eden, seemed to read something in his face that she had never seen there before. Beth had spent eighteen years of her life on one of the outer islands. She had seen human nature in the raw there, and she was under no delusions about it. But she had also read about romantic love in novels, and how it came upon one unaware.

That was why, during the journey to Sydney, which had been ended by the burning and beaching of the *Olympia,* she had fallen in love with Freddy. She had built up a romantic creation out that love. Then she had seen Freddy trying to shoot Eden in the back, and had seen him helpless in the hands of this great man, with the red hair on his chest, who could knock men cold with single blows of his mighty fists.

But it was something of pity and tenderness in Eden's face that suddenly told Beth the truth.

"It's you I love—it's you," she whispered.

Red Eden let out a roar, and then he struck her across the face and sent her reeling. Freddy didn't utter a sound. Beth came back slowly. A little blood trickled from the corner of her mouth. "It's you I love," she repeated.

"I'm taking you both to Sydney," boomed Eden suddenly. "You can get married there, or you can go to hell. I'm locking you in the cabin, Beth Tyson. You, Freddy, will bunk with George in the bow. Get down! Get down, I tell you!"

THE slight tide of the islands was cresting the treacherous submerged reef with a line of foam.

The schooner lifted on the surge and passed out into the sea. Eden stood with one arm about the lithe form of the Polynesian girl. In his other hand he held a nearly empty bottle. Slowly the dawn was eating up the darkness.

Down in the cabin he heard Beth hammering with her fists again and calling for Freddy. Freddy was neatly trussed up, to keep him out of harm until Pango Island was out of vision. Eden let out that gargantuan laugh of his, and drew Marya closer to him. He had dreamed for a night, but this was reality, straddling the deck, with a girl beside him, and enough copra for a wild honeymoon a little later.

Invitation to Romance

[Continued from page 47]

"Until the man comes back with a loaded pistol, and perhaps with someone to help him. That's why you want to keep me here."

She drew back, staring at him. "I— Why should I . . . ?"

"I don't pretend to understand it," he said. "But you lifted the pistols from my sash while we were in the carriage. If you had done that simply for the sake of comfort you wouldn't have forgotten and left them in the carriage, knowing we might be attacked. And you called me across the dark doorsill to be killed. And the money isn't hidden here. And the perfume's wrong."

"The money—" A pulse began to beat in the hollow between her breasts. "Where—?"

"There's a lot I don't understand. But I will feel safer in my own quarters. Let's go."

"No! I—" She tried to leap away, and his hand closed on her wrist. With the flat of his sword he struck playfully at the swelling curve of her thigh. "Are you coming willingly?" He was still smiling, still with that one eyebrow lifted, but after a moment of staring into his face she said:

"I will go willingly."

THEY went in the carriage with Charles Lane driving and the girl on the seat beside him. Once, glancing down at her, he sighed and said, "I was tempted to stay and play—and get shot at. It would have been worth the danger, almost. Only death is such a drastic price to pay, because persons tell me that the sort of things I enjoy most are frowned upon in heaven."

The girl said nothing. In the darkness he could not see her face well enough even to guess at what she was thinking.

The carriage rolled into the courtyard of his house and he waited a moment, but there was no sign of Horsehair. So he jumped down and helped the girl. Together they crossed the courtyard and entered his house—and stopped dead, staring.

The girl who waited there was tall and slender and her hair was burnished red. Lane held his breath staring at her, afraid to breathe, afraid to blink because the girl might change. It didn't seem possible she could be as beautiful as she was: the kind of beauty he liked; there was nothing ethereal or saintly about her loveliness: it was the beauty of flesh and blood and full-bodied emotions. Here was a girl, Charles Lane thought, that if a man once made love to he would remember.

But she wasn't looking at Lane. She and the brunette who had come with Lane were staring at one another. "You!" the redhaired girl said, and all at once fear began to come in her face.

The brunette caught Lane's arm. "My uncle's wife!" she cried. "What is she doing here?" Her face was drawn as she stared up at Lane. "Did you know . . . .? Were you helping them all the time?"

"You are lying!" the redhaired girl cried. She swung toward Lane. "What is she doing here? Were you helping them trap me?"

"There seems to be some confusion," Lane said, "at least on my part. You two girls seem to know one another, but just what is the connection between you?"

"She is my Uncle Phillipe's wife," the brunette said. "The uncle who escaped."

The redhaired girl gaped at her, then Lane. "She's lying. Her name is Adrienne Delacroix, and she is married to one of my uncles."

"Wait a minute," Lane said. "Just which one of you has been writing me these letters?"

Both girls said, "I have."

"Such popularity!" Lane said, grinning; then, speaking directly between the two, "But Mademoiselle Janice—" and paused.

Both girls said, "What is it?"

"I seem to be hearing double," Lane said. He repeated the brunette's story about her uncles and the fortune that was legally hers. "What's your opinion of that?" he asked the redhead.

"The story is true," she said. "Except that I am the niece, and this woman married my Uncle Phillipe a year ago. Since then they have kept a closer watch than ever on me. They have rarely let me leave the house and have watched me everywhere I went. I knew that I could never get justice in New Orleans, and living here is like living in jail. But I managed to get some of the gold and jewels that are rightfully mine and send them to you. I hoped that you would see me safely on the ship which sails tomorrow. W i t h o u t protection, even if I managed to reach the ship, my uncles would take me off again."

"It's a lie!" the brunette said. "She is Adrienne. I am Janice."

"The choice seems to be left to me," Lane said. He crossed to the redhaired girl and, calmly, leaned and kissed her. He breathed deeply. "The right perfume," he said. "The perfume that was on the letters. The local tea-olive, and my favorite odor. I have decided, mademoiselle, that you are whom you claim to be."

A MAN'S voice said, "You have guessed correctly, monsieur, but too late. Dead men cause no trouble to those who do not dream —and I never dream."

The man was tall and thin, with the face of a hawk. The pistol he held was pointed steadily at Charles Lane. His forefinger curled tight around the trigger.

Lane bowed. His face showed nothing but police interest but his heart was pounding, his muscles contracting as though by growing hard they could stop the bullet from entering.

"Uncle Phillipe, I presume?"

"Correct." The man's finger began to tighten on the trigger. "And now, if you are ready to die—"

"But I'm not!" Lane cried. "I see no profit in it. Certainly nothing for me, and nothing for you that I know about."

"No profit," the hawkfaced man said, "but security. We found Janice's last letter before her maid brought it to you. Just how much she had told you previously, we didn't know. But the letter said you had never seen her, so I locked Janice where I thought she would not escape and sent Adrienne on to bring you where—we thought—it would be easy to dispose of you. You proved tougher than we had suspected, and while I was gone Janice's maid helped her to escape. I thought she might come here; so I followed."

"That makes it all very clear," Lane said.

"And now—" again the finger began to tighten on the trigger.

"Wait!" Lane cried. "Wait!" Half the room separated him from Phillipe. The pistols were in his sash, but to try to draw one meant death.

And then a curtain moved on the far side of the room. Horsehair, the slave, stood there, blinking stupidly at the man with the gun. Phillipe Delacroix's finger was white around the trigger, tightening slowly, steadily.

"Wait!" Lane cried again. "If you shoot me, monsieur, my servant who is directly behind you, is going to be forced to put that knife between your shoulders."

Phillippe Delacroix laughed. "I am not fool enough to believe that. And now—"

It all happened in the same instant. Horsehair said, "Ah's really here, sur, but I ain't got no knife. I—" Phillipe Delacroix was whirling. Gun thunder shook the room. One of the girls screamed. Horsehair stood gaping, unmoving. Smoke drifted upward from the muzzle of Charles Lane's pistol to form a pale blue question mark in the air.

Phillipe Delacroix lay face down upon the wine colored carpet.

LATER, when it was dawn outside and a light mist hung over the city, when Phillipe Delacroix's body had been removed and the brunette Adrienne had gone also, Charles Lane asked Horsehair where he had been when he (Lane) arrived in the carriage with Adrienne. "Why didn't you come to look after the horses?" he asked.

"You come in er car'age sho nuff?" Horsehair said. "Ah reckon Ah musta been too busy to heah anythin' small's a horse, sur." His face shone suddenly like a full moon when he grinned. "Dat French gal wuz sho hard to reach, but she do respond when caught up wid! Man-man!"

"Probably I should do something about you," Lane said; "but you did arrive just in time to save my life. So get on back to your quarters and see that M'amselle Delacroix's maid is made comfortable."

"Dat's de job fer me," Horsehair said. "An' does I do a good job uf it!"

Lane went back into the room where Janice Delacroix waited. The candles were still burning, but the light of early dawn made their flames paler than the girl's hair. "It has been a strenuous night," he said. He poured burgundy into crystal glasses.

"To the end of danger," she said.

"And the beginning of romance."

She smiled, and drank, her eyes that were sometimes green, sometimes almost golden, watching Lane over the glass.

"I would like to thank you, monsieur, if I only knew how."

"Oh you know how," Lane said. His eyes were laughing now, his heart beginning to pound. He had known many beautiful women, but here in the light of the guttering candles and the misty dawn he did not think he had ever seen one as beautiful as the redhaired girl beside him.

"There is no need for you to leave New Orleans now," he said. "Where your uncles have gone they will not trouble you any more."

"My home is really my own now," she said.

"Yes," Lane said. "But there is no need to hurry back to it. Is there?"

The girl drained the last of her wine. He could see the smooth skin above her breasts rise and fall with her breathing, the flesh white and satin-like and glowing. Her eyes were almost black. She leaned toward him, and as his arms went around her, his lips came down on hers, she whispered, panting, "No need to hurry—now."

The Laughing Moor

[Continued from page 71]

Past the General's Palace, with its deserted halls. But in the guard-room of the Citadel the other dozen of troopers were thrusting on their armor. They shouted in amazement at the sight of Muley Hassan and Francis, and the eight troopers, with blood dripping from their armor-joints.

Francis cried, "Our lord Muley Hassan is now the lawful King of Granada. Who fights for him? Who fights?"

They yelled, raising the points of their scimitars. Francis shouted:

"Back along the ramparts! Call on the troops! Back into the Alhambra! Death to the usurper, Boabdil!"

He might have had the game in his hands some fifteen minutes before, but he had lost it now.

HE SAW that, as there came another charge of the palace guards, crossbowmen at their head, whose quarrels clanged on the corselets of the guards, and sent chips of stone flying from the Alcazaba doors. Behind them came a phalanx of pikemen, roaring along the ramparts. Francis and Muley Hassan leaped to the front to meet the charge, and the yelling troopers followed them, cutting down the guards and turning them back to flight.

But there came another charge, and another, and the numbers of the defenders were growing pitifully fewer under the quarrels and the strokes of the pikes. They were being driven back now into the great guard-room of the Citadel.

But still Alayne was at Francis's shoulder, and he looked at her and laughed again. This death was better than at the hands of Englishmen on Bosworth Field.

Once more Francis and Muley

Hassan led their men against the attacking phalanx. The old Moor's arm was weary now, but the scimitar of the Englishman lopped through mail and flesh.

There were a bare half-dozen left to resist the attack of the royal forces, whose men were strewn in groaning, writhing ridges upon the ground. Behind them was the open door of the guard-house; at the further end the great oaken one behind which were the mysterious, unknown depths of the ancient Citadel. The guard-room itself was bare, straw-littered, and indefensible.

The six stood panting in the entrance, awaiting the next attack. It came with surge of pike and scimitar, and once more Boabdil's men recoiled before the three remaining defenders.

These were Muley Hassan, whose stout armor had protected him, Francis, and the sub-captain. At Francis's shoulder, as ever, Alayne. A quarrel had grazed her cheek in its flight, and there was a little trickle of blood there, but otherwise she was uninjured.

Now a new troop of crossbowmen was coming up. Their missiles clanged on the Alcazaba walls; one struck Francis upon the corselet and sent him staggering back into Alayne's arms.

He sprang forward and dragged back Muley Hassan. He closed the great doors of the guard-house and had flung the bolts into their sockets before the enemy perceived his manoeuvre. Inside it was almost dark. Outside there came a furious hammering as the royal troops strove to gain admittance.

Francis looked at Muley Hassan, and drew from his pouch the great key to the interior of the Alcazaba, that he had never used.

Did Muley Hassan know the secret exit down the precipice?

If they could find it, and convey Alayne through the Moorish lines that night, to Santa Fé, there would be freedom and happiness for her. For himself—?

A grim smile curled Francis's lips as he thought of the fate in store for him.

CHAPTER VIII

The Stake

FRANCIS turned the great key in the ancient lock, and heard the harsh grating of metal. The door swung slowly open, as if propelled by a blast of air from within. On the outer door of the guard-house the royal troops were hammering furiously, but they would have to bring beams or rocks before it could be forced.

Francis looked down into a pit of blackness. There was no longer daylight, nor any light inside the Citadel.

Muley Hassan clutched at his arm. "She is here," he babbled. "She must have heard the tumult, and fled. There is a secret hiding-place where we can lie—food in it, too. I have seen to it. I have prepared against this day."

Francis saw then that he did not know of the passage-way, which Zorayah had probably herself discovered during her long years of imprisonment, as the slave of the old man's desires.

"We must hide where they cannot find us. Later we may be able to find a way out of the Alhambra," babbled the old man. "You, who slew my son Yussef, why should I love you still? Ah, it is like that day aboard my galley, when you fought like a lion at my side. I am old and broken now, and a mockery in the eyes of the Moorish people."

Foot by foot they felt their way down a flight of stone steps, Francis holding Alayne. Far overhead there sounded a terrific crash as the outer doors of the guard-room yielded. Now they were squeezing through a rocky passage. But there remained only Muley Hassan, Francis, and Alayne.

Muley Hassan stooped in the darkness. A stone turned, a little light appeared. Then Francis saw that they were in a long rock chamber, and the light was that of the moon, coming through an archer's cleft in a wall.

The old man moved the stone again, and now there was no sound from above.

"We are safe now. Soon Zorayah will come," whispered Muley Hassan, as he dropped on the stone floor.

FRANCIS sank down, heavy with sleep, but he felt Alayne's hand in his. "You have forgiven me?" he whispered.

Her fingers tightened against his in answer, and he knew that Granada was a dream, and there was nothing but the close of Castle Eastover, and the white roses. He slept, Alayne in his arms.

Then suddenly a scream from Muley Hassan, an answering scream from Alayne brought him to his feet, dazed and bewildered.

REPLENISHING JESSICA — Maxwell Bodenheim

CONFLICT of LOVE and DESIRE

■ The story of a young woman, full of passion and the love of life. The conflict between lust and the spirit makes sensational reading that holds you spell-bound until the last page is finished. Reformers tried in vain to prohibit its publication. Seventeen complete editions were sold at the original price of $2.

THE TIME OF HER LIFE — Cornell Woolrich

TAMED by the ONE MAN

■ This $10,000 prize-winning author has writen the amazing story of a very young, very alluring, very ruthless adventuress. Her mother had been the gay and reckless "Grass Widow" whose mad love of pleasure she had inherited. Her life became a veil of deceit concealing wild escapades with rich and pleasure-sated men-about-town until, in the final pages, she is tamed by *the* man. Even at $2 this was a "Best Seller."

PLAYTHINGS OF DESIRE — J. Wesley Putnam

A STORY of PASSION

■ The flaming fire of a great and overpowering love in a smashing story that swings the glittering lights of Broadway to the sanctity of the North Woods. A strong emotional heart-stirring novel of a rich roué and his wife and the rugged Big Woods guide who proves more sophisticated than was expected. The frank answer to the question "What does a faithful wife owe an unfaithful husband?" Many $2 editions of this "best seller" were sold out.

EACH BOOK ILLUSTRATED above in ORIGINAL FORMAT and BINDING has been REPRINTED and BOUND in MAGAZINE STYLE!

YOU can have all 6 for 98¢ PLUS POSTAGE

A VIRTUOUS GIRL — Maxwell Bodenheim

STARK DRAMA of ENDURING LOVE

■ The passionate story of Emmy-Lou . . . wistful, pink-and-white Emmy-Lou, 17 respectable years old in the corseted era of 1900. Alluring, born to love under the spell of a summer night and a boy whom her parents forbade. They called her "fast" in Chicago but Emmy-Lou believed in Romance and was ready to pay for it. A pulse-quickening drama of a girl's courage against the strangling conventions of respectability! Formerly $2.

THE MARRIAGE GUEST — Konrad Bercovici

REVOLT AGAINST CONVENTIONS

■ The tale of a vicarious love of a fine, sensitive woman who has succumbed to the necessities of existence and conventionality, but whose fine spirit to the end, lives with, is loved by and bears children for the man she really loves. Stark drama of the crucifixion of three lives, through which runs the golden thread of a woman's passionate, enduring love, defying the world. $2 worth of intense drama!

BROADWAY RACKETEERS — John O'Connor

THE LUSTS of the RACKET MOBS

■ A masterpiece of the Main Stem by the Bernard Shaw of Broadway. You get both sides of the racket, plus the laughs and lusts of the racket mob, told in the jargon of Racketyland. Never before has Broadway artifice, in all its phases, blazing with illicit loves, honeycombed with intrigue, teeming with swift-paced lives, been exposed to the light as in this volume. Real life characters with authentic data exactly as originally sold in its $2 edition.

Hours of Exciting Reading for Less Than $1.00!

SENSATIONAL NOVELS BY MASTERS OF FICTION NOT ONE WORD OMITTED

■ Think of it—six books of thrilling fiction—all recent "best sellers"—for *less than half* the price of *one* of them! These six daring books by famous authors are so enthralling, so gripping, that the public made them "best sellers" at $2. Every one is packed with romance and mystery, passion and intrigue . . . spell-binding in its fast moving action . . . that extra something that it takes to make people clamor for a copy!

EACH BOOK IS COMPLETE, BOUND SEPARATELY AND UNEXPURGATED

■ Each book—shown above as photographed in its original $2 binding—has been reprinted in clear, easily-read type on pages 6⅜ x 9⅜ inches and bound in magazine style. The attractive, heavy paper covers are alike so that the 6 books form a handsome set for your library. Not one word has been left out! Hours of exciting entertainment are yours . . . for only 98c!

TAKE ADVANTAGE OF THIS ASTOUNDING OFFER NOW!

■ We are able to make you this astonishing offer only because of our tremendous volume of sales and because we want to introduce the Mayfair Editions of "best sellers" to new readers at this low price!

EDITION LIMITED . . . MAIL COUPON NOW!

MAYFAIR PUBLISHING CO.
1270 Sixth Ave., Dept. 1111, New York, N. Y.

Please send me the six best sellers. I will pay the postman 98c, plus a few cents postage on delivery. If I am not completely satisfied I will return the books within five days and the full purchase price will be refunded immediately.

Name..........

Address..........

City.......... State..........

If you enclose $1 with this coupon we will pay all postage charges. Canadian Orders $1.25 in advance. Foreign orders 6 shillings in advance.

ONLY FAMOUS "BEST SELLERS" ARE INCLUDED!

Every book selected for its record of popularity. We are so sure you will be delighted with these books that we guarantee to return your purchase price in five days if you are not completely satisfied. Don't miss this chance . . . send the coupon today while they last! You can't lose!

MAYFAIR PUBLISHING CO., Radio City, 1270 SIXTH AVENUE, NEW YORK, N. Y.

SATISFACTION GUARANTEED OR MONEY IMMEDIATELY REFUNDED

A veiled figure rushed at him with a screech. A point of steel pierced his shoulder and sent him staggering back. He saw the half bare, voluptuous breasts of Zorayah.

She vanished somewhere in the gloom. Francis ran to Muley Hassan. A spout of blood was bursting from between the joints of his armor. The old man moaned and writhed; his head fell back, and he lay still.

That was the end of the ex-King of Granada's infatuation for the woman who had cost him his throne—that dagger-thrust between the joints of his armor.

Francis bent over the dead man, then took Alayne in his arms. "There is a way down to the Vega somewhere," he said.

They went through the darkness, and they palmed the great stone, working over it with their finger-tips. But the secret of the entrance seemed to have died with Muley Hassan.

Then of a sudden the tramp of steel-shod men echoed through the chamber. Tramp, tramp, files of them, companies of them. The hollow walls seemed to resound to the stamp and scuffle of those steel-shod legions. And then of a sudden the rock chamber was filled with armed men.

Francis and Alayne were forced apart. They were borne upward by the press, through a passage of which Francis had been ignorant. High overhead a fight was raging. At last Francis stood upon the ramparts in the moonlight.

In front of him, Spaniards and Moors were engaged in a furious battle. The serried phalanxes of Aragon and Castile were hurling themselves upon the defenders of the Alhambra, who came charging on with swinging scimitars. And all along the ramparts sulverins were belching fire and lead at the legions that were assaulting the mighty Moorish citadel.

Surprised, bewildered by the enemies assailing them from every point, the Moors broke and fled. In front of the Alhambra the remnants of their forces were being cut down by the long Spanish swords.

Out of the Alhambra, those two fantastic puppet-figures were being led, to pass into Africa. The kingdom of the Moors in Spain was ended.

"Now, had I known that Aragon and Castile possessed such warriors, I might have thrown in my lot with them," said Francis to the officer who had him in charge.

"We keep a stout, fire-blackened stake for heretics and renegades."

THE long speech of the Procurator bored King Ferdinand, while Queen Isabella yawned behind her fan. This Don Gregorio was old, which was unfortunate in those days of youth, but he was a bore too. Besides, the fate of the young man had been decided in advance.

So felt King Ferdinand, who cut Don Gregorio short in his final peroration.

"The case stands thus," he said. "The accused, being of Christian birth, joined with the paynim Moors to fight for Granada. What have you to say to that, Francis Blount?"

"I have never been a convert to the religion of the paynim," said

Francis, "but served them as a Mozarebe."

"That must be admitted," said the Archbishop of Talavera reluctantly.

"I love him," said Alayne, rising from beside the Queen. "Sire, he fled from England, because he fought for the late King Richard. Since then he has wandered in the lands of the Moors, to which he was trepanned, not knowing that there is now an amnesty in England, to which he may return—"

Young Sir Philip, spruce in his padded doublet, of the new fashion, tried to pull her down.

"Moreover, he is a kinsman of my father's, as I call my father to witness."

"Well, yes," said Baron Eastover, distressed, but diplomatic. "The young man is, in truth, a distant kinsman of mine, yet I am not disposed to assail your Majesty's judgment."

"We love each other," said Alayne again.

Queen Isabella smiled. "Should not that be enough?" she asked. "Is not this a veritable miracle, that love should endure? Give the young man back to her, sire, since nothing is proved against him."

Ferdinand threw up his hands. It was hard enough to be the husband of a queen in her own right, without bothering his head about legal points.

Francis, amazed, felt Alayne's tremulous touch upon his arm. He looked incredulously into her eyes. Then he knew that the white and red roses still bloomed on the trellises at Castle Eastover.

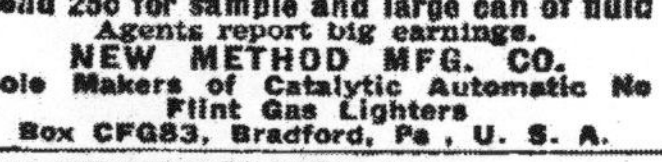

Swamp Princess

[Continued from page 81]

dragged into another room. His hands were tied.

PRESENTLY, partially recovering from the blow, he discovered another form next to his own in the darkness.

"Who are you?" a harsh whisper reached him.

"Pete Garner, New Orleans reporter. And you're John Somers?"

"Yes."

"Are you tied up, too?"

"Yes."

"But you have your teeth! Listen—they have your daughter in there!"

"Sally? Good God!"

"She has the tender mercy of two swamp rats and that Cajun she-devil. You know what that means. Now listen—I'll try to get my wrists to your mouth and you work on the knots—before it's too late."

Somers wasted no breath on words then . . . even when, after a few minutes, they both heard Sally's cry of fear and despair from the other room. . . .

Another cry, and a loud, triumphant laugh from one of the swampmen . . . and now Pete's hands were free. He scrambled to his feet, swayed groggily for a moment; then, disregarding Somers' plea to untie him, Pete tried the door. Apparently they had thought it safe enough not to lock in their bound prisoners, for the door opened easily and Pete Garner blinked in the lamplight.

Sally struggled weakly, across the room, in the bestial embrace of Pierre Valois, who had ripped her dress completely away and tossed it aside. Between the flimsy protections of the girl's step-ins and bandeau, her fair skin was reddened harshly from the brutal grasping of her assailant's roughened hands. Desperately, her legs threshed and her knees punched at Pierre's body, but he seemed only to enjoy her resistance, for a broad grin distended his bearded lips.

All this Pete saw in a fraction of a second, just as he saw Etienne standing by, grinning. There was no trace of Madelon to be seen.

WITH a bellow of rage, Pete sprang. And instantly Etienne snatched a knife from his belt and threw it. The point ripped into Pete's coat sleeve, slicing through to the hilt. He felt only a sting at the slight cut, but he stopped suddenly and jerked the knife out as Pierre flung Sally's figure to the floor and the two swampmen bore down on him.

Side-stepping, he plunged the knife to the hilt into the side of Pierre Valois and, as the man stumbled, tripping his comrade, Pete grabbed the flailing right arm of Etienne with his own left hand and stepped back, pulling with all his might. His feet blocked by the fallen Pierre's body, Etienne pitched forward and sidewise with sharp momentum. Before his enemy's body had struck the floor,

Pete allowed himself to drop on top of him, his right forearm extended, so that the bone, near the elbow, was against the other's throat.

The back of Etienne's head smacked the floor viciously, and at the same instant all Pete's weight was thrown into the elbow held at the man's throat. There was a sharp crunch of cartilage and an agonized groan from Etienne. Pete saw blood welling from the Cajun's mouth, then, but the unconscious man didn't move. He was choking on his own blood. . . .

Rising to his feet, with brief mental thanks for the luck that had allowed him to dispose of both men in so short a time, he turned to the sobbing girl kneeling where Pierre had dropped her.

"Sally!" he whispered. "Come—we must get your father out of here quickly."

He lifted her in his arms and stumbled into the rear room, where John Somers had managed to squirm almost to the open door.

A MINUTE later, half supporting Sally and her freed father, Pete hurried them out of the cabin.

"My pirogue!" he gasped. "It'll hold three. We'll send someone back to capture the woman. God knows where she is. Hiding in the swamp probably."

But she wasn't hiding. They had barely shoved off in the pirogue when into the dim spot of moonlight drenching the mudbank stepped Madelon. "Stop!" she snarled. "Stop or I'll shoot the girl!"

Pete raised his hands and the paddle disappeared over the side and drifted away. "Come back, quickly!" the Cajun queen said tensely. "Or I shall kill you all. Even"—she added viciously—"as I shall kill those two for letting you escape the minute I step outside to leave them alone with the girl."

"You won't have to kill them," Pete told her. "I did it for you."

"You *what?*"

"They're dead, both of them. And now if you want us back, you'll have to reach me a pole. You made me lose our only paddle when I put up my hands."

"*Oui!* I shall bring you back so that I may cut out that girl's heart before your eyes. You I shall kill more slowly, *M'sieu* Murderer!"

Picking up a stripped, dead

branch from the bank, she extended it to Pete Garner, and as his hand gripped it he jerked.

THERE was a sharp cry from the woman, a roar from her gun as a bullet ploughed into the gunwale of the pirogue. Madelon swayed wildly on the slippery mudbank and splashed into the black waters of the swamp.

"Quick!" barked Pete. "Get her. We'll take her back somehow."

But moving the pirogue with the branch he still held was clumsy business, and he never got her. For suddenly a log rose out of the water and the Cajun woman screamed in terror. The log was an alligator. There was a whipping threshing movement of the water and both 'gator and woman disappeared.

"God!" Pete stared at the black swamp, motionless as cold sweat dewed his face. She was a very devil, that woman, but she was a woman; and evil as she had been, her passions had stirred Pete Garner during the brief minute he had held her in his arms. All that voluptuous beauty, being torn now to bloody shreds in the depths of the swamp. . . . Pete shivered. Beside him, Sally moaned and covered her face with her hands.

"Forget about her, darling," he said harshly. He took off his coat and covered the girl with it, and, numbly, she lifted her mouth for his comforting kiss. "From now on," he said, "all we need to remember is—you and me."

He poled the pirogue toward the drifting paddle.

Glory's Epitaph

[Continued from page 27]

screamed when I put the pressure to his eyeballs. His yellow came to the surface. "*Gott . . . nein* . . . not that. . . !" he yowled.

I pressed harder; felt the eyeballs so soft under my thumbs. I felt the slippery fluid bursting out of them, running down his cheeks, wetting my own palms. "Now, damn your soul!" I rasped. I measured him; gave him my fist, full to the whining slobber of his loose mouth.

Blood sprayed me. Von Kragg's blood. He tried to go down. I wouldn't let him. I propped him against the wall and battered his face to a crimson smear. Then, when I realized that he wasn't feeling my punches any longer because he was unconscious, I hurled him out the window.

I was just insane enough to enjoy hearing his body burst open against the alley paving. . . .

FROM the hallway, somebody was smashing at the bedroom door with a chair; splintering the panels. I had no time to lose, now. I lifted Emy in my arms, flung her over my shoulder. She clung weakly to me as I worked myself over the windowsill. She whispered: "No . . . you cannot do it . . . leave me here and save yourself. . . ."

I held her more tightly with my left arm. With my right hand I clung to the improvised rope. We dangled there until I could get the rope worked around my legs as a snubbing brake. Then I lowered myself and my moaning feminine burden.

We gained the alley at long last. By that time, that bedroom door had been battered open. Someone was leaning out the window. A gun lanced spiteful red flame.

Twisting, zig-zagging, I raced for the mouth of the alley with Emy in my arms. Far in the distance I heard the peculiar yip-yipping sirens used by Continental police-cars. I darted across the street to another alley. Then I stopped for a moment in the shadowy concealment there. I had to stop. I was just about done. I couldn't carry Emy any longer. Not until I'd rested a moment.

I lowered her. She swayed against me. "You must go on . . . alone!" she said brokenly.

"Never!"

She said: "But . . . you *must!* I am . . . dying. . . ."

Then I saw the blood. A sickened feeling reached its tentacles into my heart. "You're shot!"

She nodded. "That bullet . . . from Von Kragg's gun . . . the one that broke the mirror . . . it passed . . . through my body . . . first. . . ."

"God!" I said. "You threw yourself in front of his automatic to save my life!"

NEW YORK / 25¢
BEHIND the SCENES

A smile came wanly to her lips. "It did not . . . matter . . . because I had no desire . . . to live . . . after . . . what happened. . . ." she turned her head away from me. "I could not hope . . . to win your love . . . any more. . . ."

She was wrong. It wouldn't have made any difference to me. I tried to tell her so. Not with words, but with the kiss I pressed gently upon her lips and the fondling caress I gave her.

A vague shudder coursed through her flesh. She smiled again, wistfully. "Thank you for . . . everything, *Herr* Kenthorne," she said. Then her eyes closed. She became a limp weight in my embrace.

I felt for her heart. It was no longer beating.

Well, at least I had repaid Von Kragg. And so I left Emy lying there in that alley; made my way toward safety. With luck, I'd be meeting Gollancz Dresca in Paris within a few days. His sister had died to save his life and mine. In my heart, that will always be her epitaph.

But there are times when I think of her, and of the things that might have been.

Diamonds Under the Sea

[Continued from page 89]

"Fasten it to the line. We'll haul it up; then take care of you."

Madison grinned sardonically to himself. They'd take care of him, all right! He took grim pleasure in his uncompromising answer. "Bring me up if you want your package."

After a moment he felt himself being drawn upward.

And then out of nowhere he saw again that gray, shadowy shape that had given him chills before. He could see it clearly through the glass plate in his helmet, a monstrous white-bellied shark, its ugly, serrated jaws wide. If it fouled his air-hose. . . .

He didn't hesitate. The knife in his hand licked out with lightning speed. The sharp blade sliced into the creature's gross belly. The water around him reddened and was churned into sudsy foam. And at the same time his ascent quickened.

Too fast! The pressure on his diving suit was falling off dangerously fast. The sun-lit waters were brightening. His ear-drums ached and blood trickled from his nose from the too rapid lessening of pressure. Then he realized he was out in the air.

French and Geist pulled him onto the platform. He felt a blow on his wrist as one of them struck the knife from his grasp. The metal container was torn from him. Dazedly he saw an automatic in Simon French's hand trained on him.

He managed to grin in the face of the gun's threat. French stared at him, at the box's trick lock. He put down the gun and unscrewed Madison's helmet. "What's the combination?" he shouted, too excited apparently to realize that opening the box could be accomplished by knocking the lock off.

Madison still grinned.

French thrust the box in his hand. "Open it!"

MADISON, heart beating like mad, answered casually: "Help me out of this rig. My fingers are stiff."

Geist picked up the knife that Madison had dropped and ripped the outfit away.

Deftly Madison spun the tiny dial. The lid opened. "Just a minute," he said sharply. "If you want your package, there's another container inside this one."

Open-mouthed, but watching him with cat-like intensity, they waited while Madison fumbled inside the outer shell. Water sloshed on his fingers. He prayed that it hadn't penetrated all the way.

Slowly he got it open and his hand went through the second opening. He pushed Geist's package to one side and his fingers found the grip of an automatic.

Madison didn't take time to aim. But his slug smashed the first mate's wrist that held the gun. Then Madison swung his weapon to cover both the conspirators. "June! June!" he shouted.

THE girl took in the situation at a glance. She raced down the deck and picked up French's automatic. While she covered the two of them, Madison lashed them separately to the rail.

There was triumph in the look he turned on the girl. "Between the two of us, we should be able to run this tub back to San Diego," he told her. "There's no hurry now."

THEY were standing arm in arm in the pilot cabin, nearing San Diego, when she said, "Paul, darling, I have a confession to make."

He answered abstractedly. "Yes?"

"It's about a lie I told you. About how I happened to be in that hotel where Geist and French were plotting."

He drew her closer. "There is nothing you need to tell me."

"But I want to. I didn't just happen to be there. I was following Geist. You see, I'm a detective, and my firm had been hired to find the diamonds."

Madison laughed aloud. "What does it matter? You got the diamonds. That was your job. I have evidence that will clear me of having lost the *Avatar*. That was my big job in life. Now, together, we're going to undertake a new job, an even bigger job. That is, if you'll be my wife."

He found his answer in her eyes.

Made in the USA
Lexington, KY
10 July 2019